A

VIOLENT

GOSPEL

PRAISE FOR
A VIOLENT GOSPEL
BY MARK WESTMORELAND

"Let me be the first to sing *A Violent Gospel*'s praises. Mark Westmoreland's debut is the literary equivalent of The Dukes of Hazzard driving onto the set of Elmore Leonard's Jus-tified. This book is filled with folks who know right from wrong but don't like boring."

> —**David Tromblay**, author of *As You Were*
> and *Sangre Road*

"Mark Westmoreland's *A Violent Gospel* is a down-n-dirty, rough-n-tumble romp where no punches are pulled, and Old Testament justice is the law of the land."

> —**Steph Post**, author of *Lightwood* and *Miraculum*

"In *A Violent Gospel* Mark Westmoreland stakes his claim as a powerful voice in the Neo-Southern Gothic Movement. Equal parts Flannery O'Connor, Harry Crews with a smidge of Gator era Burt Reynolds, *A Violent Gospel* is a visceral slice of existential cornbread."

> —**S.A. Cosby**, The New York Times Best Selling author of
> *Razorblade Tears* and *Blacktop Wasteland*

"This book is rural crime fiction at its best. A bullet read that gets right down to the dark and dirty point. Westmoreland's ability to play in the gray area between darkness and light is spot on word candy that is perfectly suited to the title of *A Violent Gospel*. Look out for this guy. He's going to listed with Daniel Woodrell and Tom Franklin in no time."

> —**Brian Panowich**, author of *Hard Cash Valley*
> and *Bull Mountain*

"*A Violent Gospel* is one rollicking old testament ass whoopin' of a debut. Westmoreland is an exciting new voice in southern noir, delivering 100 Proof Hellbilly Pulp and I can't wait for more."

> —**Peter Farris**, author of *Last Call for the Living*
> and *Clay Eaters*

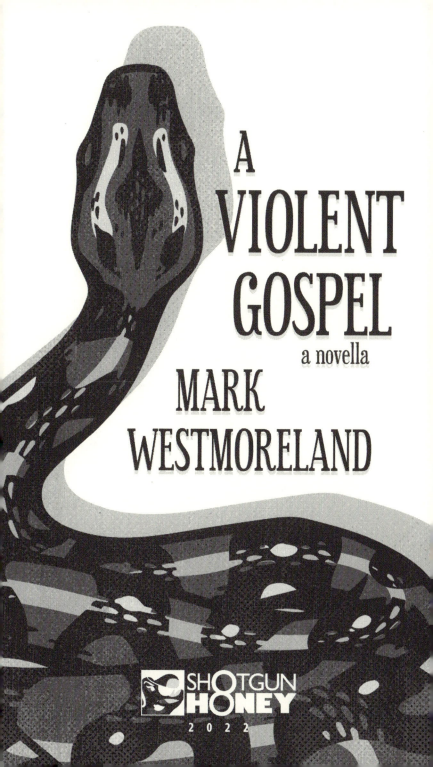

A VIOLENT GOSPEL

a novella

MARK WESTMORELAND

SHOTGUN H8NEY
2022

Shotgun Honey
215 Loma Road
Charleston, WV 25314
www.ShotgunHoney.com

Cover Design by Bad Fido.

First Printing 2021.

ISBN-10: 1-956957-03-0
ISBN-13: 978-1-956957-03-7

10 9 8 7 6 5 4 3 2   22 21 20 19 18 17

For Dawn,
You make all the words worth it.

A VIOLENT GOSPEL

And from the days of John the Baptist until now the kingdom of heaven suffereth violence, and the violent take it by force.

Matthew 11:12 (KJV)

PART ONE

Bringing in the sheaves, bringing in the sheaves
We shall come rejoicing, bringing in the sheaves
Brining in the sheaves, bringing in the sheaves
We shall come rejoicing, bringing in the sheaves

1.

Rusted strands of barbed wire were the only obstacles keeping us from sneaking onto the Lewellen property. The cords had gotten weathered by the elements and hung limp in the fence posts, so they pulled up easy when I grabbed them. Marshall dropped to the ground and crawled on his belly the way an infantryman does on the battlefield. Once he got to the other side, he dusted himself off, took the fencing from me, and I snaked my way through. If Harper Lewellen caught us trespassing, he'd get mad enough to shit bullet holes through us.

It wasn't my idea to sneak onto old Harp's property. He'd hated me ever since I was a kid in high school. Harper caught me finger-banging his daughter one time and told me he'd shoot me if he ever saw my face again. Up to this point, I'd steered clear of him and any gun he'd aim in my direction. But Marshall told me there was something I needed to see and pestered the devil out of me until I agreed to come.

It was the dead of night, and we'd counted on there being enough moonlight to see in the dark. I'd told Marshall there wasn't no way I was sneaking around

Harp's with a flashlight. The only problem is I didn't consider the forecast, and with it being partly cloudy, it obscured what light we could see by. After it started drizzling some, we scooted through the woods like a pair of coon dogs tracking a scent.

Marshall slowed when we reached the edge of the tree line and found a kudzu strangled hickory stump to hide behind. I camouflaged myself behind the tree next to him and waited for him to signal what to do next. Marshall was down on one knee, peering over the stump's jagged lip. I didn't know what my brother was looking for, but I was on the scope out for any Lewellen who might be stirring. It wasn't an easy task with it being well past dusk and the lack of moonlight, but I wasn't saying nothing to Marshall. He'd already given me two earfuls of shit about bringing no flashlights.

Marshall whistled to get my attention and pointed where he wanted us to go. I looked past Harper's two-story home, the double-wide his mama lived in, and way out to a sheet metal building. Before Harp caught me two knuckles deep inside Andy, she'd snuck me inside that shop a couple of times. It's where her deddy liked spending his time drinking, watching Georgia games, and rebuilding classic cars. It was that man's sanctuary, and if we got caught inside there, we'd get shot on sight.

I looked back over at Marshall and shook my head. He'd come off his heels to make a run for the building and almost fell over trying to stop. He threw his hands out to the side and mouthed something at me, even though he knew I couldn't read lips, especially in the damn dark. I threw a thumb over my shoulder to let him know I thought we should head back. Marshall wasn't having it. I knew he thought we'd come too far to turn back now, and he did the one thing I hoped he wouldn't by taking off on in a flat sprint and hauling ass for the building.

Against my better judgment, I chased Marshall's bootheels and could hardly breathe when we reached the shop. Marshall was barely winded and led me around the side to the only door there was. He pulled it open to step inside before I had the chance to ask him if he was crazy. I didn't bother asking myself the same because I already knew the answer.

I held the door open while Marshall looked for something we could use to prop it open. What we needed to do is find a light switch, but I wasn't going to waste a word telling Marshall so. We'd made a rule not to speak unless it was necessary and telling him something he already knew didn't qualify. Marshall appeared from the darkness like some horror movie slasher carrying one of Harp's tool bags he laid at the corner of the door. It moved a couple of inches when I let it go but held it, and I left the doorway.

The few times Andy brought me in here, I never paid attention to the layout of the building. She knew exactly where to lead me, and it was to her deddy's fridge for a couple of beers. We'd sit inside one of the cars he was working on, drink our cold ones, and have a backseat rodeo. I felt along the wall until my hand ran over a switch, and I flipped it. Nothing happened at first, but once the lights started buzzing, the inside of that shop lit up like the Tugalo County Titans were fixing to take the field for Friday Night Lights.

My eyes took a second to adjust, and I rubbed away the spots clouding my vision. Marshall waved for me to follow him and led me to a back corner of the building with bare walls and no tool cabinets. A steel door was sunk into the floor, and I wondered why Andy had never shown me this. Marshall dropped to a knee, lifted the door, and it opened without a squeak. Its hinges locked in place, and Marshall waved for me to follow before he dropped inside.

Marshall whistled when I didn't follow him right away and stuck his head out to see what I waited for. I didn't like the idea of not being able to keep an eye on the door. If anybody came inside, we'd be trapped with nowhere to go. But with the way Marshall looked at me, I knew there'd be no talking him out of it. We were always bent on making a series of bad decisions anyway. This wasn't no worse than some other shit we'd gotten into. Without much more thought, I followed my brother down into the hole.

2.

When my bootheels met the concrete, Marshall pulled the string on an overhead light. A single bulb lit the space enough my eyes didn't have to strain to see we were in some kind of storm shelter. I didn't know what kind of storms Harp planned on taking refuge from in north Georgia. The only tornadoes Tugalo County ever got happened while I was still wetting myself, and my only memories were of what Mama told me about them. It looked like the same thought occurred to Harper, and he turned the shelter into a bunker.

I'd never taken old Harp to be a prepper of any sort, but there were shelves lined with canned goods, emergency food rations, and store boxes of ammunition. A third World War could get started with all the firepower kept down here, but the guns were getting stored somewhere else, and aluminum storage cabinets filled the remaining wall space.

Marshall noticed me staring at the cabinets lined along the wall and put a hand on my shoulder to get my attention - then got down on a knee beside me. The doors for the cabinets were closed with a hasp - and a padlock dangled dummy locked. There wouldn't be no better time for us to leave than right now, but Marshall never got this excited unless it was on a football field. He clamped down on my shoulder, and his eyes sparkled the way they did whenever he saw some tail at the bar he wanted to grind against.

Marshall spoke for the first time all night. "This shit's fixing to get real wild, Coy. You won't never believe what old Lew's been keeping down here."

"I don't know if I wanna get involved in anything wild, Marshall. Looks like Harp's been getting ready for the end of the world."

"Don't be a pussy. He's been getting ready for more than that. Wait 'til you see."

Marshall removed one of the locks from its hasp, dropped it on the floor, and gave me one of his troublemaker smiles. Instead of jerking the door open like I thought he would, he teased it open real slow. Cash fell out in big piles at his feet, and before the door opened all the way, it was ankle-deep. Every shelf was lined with thick stacks of banded cash.

"Oh shit."

Marshall whooped, took a stack from one of the shelves, and fanned the money like some frat boy passing out singles at the Tattletale Lounge. He counted out one hundred dollar bills, let them drop to the floor, and said, "Goddamn, Coy, we're fixing to be rich."

I picked up one of the bills and held it up to the light. My mind might have been playing tricks on me, but I thought I saw Ben Franklin wink at me. I snatched the rest of the money from the floor and returned it to the cabinet.

"How'd you know all this was down here?" I asked Marshall.

"It's a long story, Coy."

"Tell it quick then."

"Wouldn't you rather take the money first?"

I'd never spent much of my life turning away free money, especially when it was getting served to me in crisp one-hundred-dollar bills, but I said, "I don't know if I wanna touch it."

"And why the hell not?" Marshall asked.

"Because you know as well as I do that Harper ain't never been nothing but country rich. He ain't never had money like this and wouldn't do nothing illegal to get it—"

"What're you trying to say?"

"He might be tied up in a situation we don't wanna get involved in."

"Well, how the hell will anybody know we took some money, Coy? There's three cabinets full here. The little bit the two of us can carry out won't even make a dent in what's left. If anybody does get suspicious about some money missing, it'll be Harper that gets the blame. Not us."

One thing I can say is that my little brother has always been able to make a hell of an argument. Enough so that we caused more trouble than we solved. Marshall's words got me thinking now, and he saw how he got to me.

"Why don't you stand there and think about it while I set aside some cash? When you're done thinking you can help me carry it out."

Marshall felt around his pockets like he was playing a game of pocket pool. "Fuck, you know what? I forgot to bring any trash bags. You did so much bitching about us not bringing flashlights I didn't think about it."

"Don't blame that shit on me, Marshall."

He waved off my words while he tried to think and said, "You think old Lew's got any in this building of his?"

"We could empty out one of his tool bags."

"You sure you don't need to think about that some more, Coy?"

I gave my brother the finger and turned to pull myself out of the hole, but cold steel nudged me backward, and I looked up into the twin barrels of a shotgun.

"What're y'all boys doing down here?"

3.

Andrea Lewellen looked down at me with the prettiest eyes. Her sandy-colored hair was pulled back into a tight ponytail like she'd never left her cheer squad behind, and she came to greet us in a thin robe that didn't do much for modesty's sake; and the way she stood above me let me enjoy the view. She caught the way I looked at her, stepped away from the edge of the hole, and aimed the shotgun at me like she remembered the day I boot-scooted all over her heart.

She switched her aim to Marshall when he stepped forward and said, "You better aim that gun somewhere else, girl."

I put a hand out for my brother to know he needed to take a backseat on this one. If anybody was going to be behind the wheel now, it ought to be me. I could charm Andy into giving me the gun and didn't think she had the sack to shoot me anyway. I might have broken her heart, but she was a resilient girl, and we recreated some memories the last time we spoke.

Marshall got the message, put his hands up, and stepped behind me. Andy let both barrels follow him and then let her aim settle back on my chest. I raised my hands to my shoulders and gave her a smile that always got her to let me push her doorbell. I guess the fog of sleep crossed her wires because her aim raised from my chest to my forehead.

I dropped the smile like I'd gotten hogtied and force-fed a gravy spoon full of mud butt. "Hey, Andy, we were just fixing to leave."

Andy looked at me with one eye over the shotgun's sight. "That ain't what I asked you. What're y'all doing down here?"

There wasn't no good way for me to answer her, and Marshall wasn't helping none poking me with a stiff finger between my shoulder blades. I knew he wanted to answer her, but I didn't trust him to be as coy as he liked thinking he was. Since my smile didn't do enough to disarm Andy, I tried humor instead. I spoke like I didn't have a care in the world. "We thought we'd just come down here for a loan."

Andy's mouth set a hard line across her face, and her features went as smooth as the porcelain dolls Mama kept locked in her curio cabinet. Marshall saw the look she gave me and spoke just loud enough for me to hear. "Goddamn, Coy, you're fixing to get us both shot."

Andy slid her feet to the left to get a better angle and aimed at Marshall over my shoulder. "What'd you say?"

Marshall answered, "I said I hope your aim ain't as good as your figure. We're both dead if it is."

She thought that was about as funny as scraping a splinter from under the skin with the dull blade of a pocketknife and let us both know it. "If y'all wanna keep standing there being funny, then I'll just go ahead and shoot you. Done got enough reason to with y'all trespassing the way y'all are."

I couldn't remember Andy ever being so thorny and thought it wiser to tread lighter. "Hey, Andy, we're just nervous with that gun being aimed at us like that. We don't mean no harm here. Ain't even got no guns on us."

I hesitated before coming clean, but she probably already knew we were unarmed, and it didn't make a difference to her anyway. She said, "Y'all oughta be nervous cause I'm this close to putting a bullet hole clear through the both of you."

Marshall stepped up. "That wouldn't be no good idea, Andy."

"And why not?"

"'Cause if you kill us, then our buddies will know we're dead, and they'll let everybody in Tugalo County know y'all got this money."

By the time Marshall finished telling his story, I'd muttered my last words and was ready to die. But when Andrea didn't pull the trigger, I started thinking I'd said them too soon.

When Marshall kept talking, it made me start doubting myself. He said, "And, Andy, we know where y'all got this money."

Hearing those words made Andy drop her aim a frog's hair and glance over her shoulder for a creep sneaking out of the dark to snatch her up. She snapped back when it didn't happen and corrected herself before we could act on it. Andy didn't stand around and try finding out how we knew where the money came from. She walked around the side of the hole and said, "I better go get Deddy."

She kicked one of the hinges, and the door slammed shut on top of us.

4.

I pushed against the door with all my strength, hoping to snap it off its lock, but the damn thing held firm. It didn't help my growth spurt came and went the same day it hit, making me a couple of inches too short to get a good hand on the door, and there wasn't anything down here I could use as a stepstool. I called Marshall over to help me, and with the two of us pushing, the door lifted a crack. We both could see just enough to know Andy wasn't nowhere around.

"That bitch locked us in here," Marshall said.

"What the hell you done got us into, Marshall?"

"Why the hell'd you tell her we didn't have no guns?"

"What were you gone do, quick draw on her?"

"Don't be a smartass, Coy."

"How 'bout you go ahead and tell me what all this is." I motioned at the cabinets full of money and the Armageddon stores even though Marshall's back was to me. "How'd you know all this was down here?"

"You know that crazy-ass church that opened up where the Dixie Mart used to be?" Marshall said. "Couple of these old dudes I work with at the shop started going not too long ago. Heard them saying they been raking in some big ass offerings every service, and one of the elders told them they escort the money here to old Lew's on Sunday afternoons."

"And how'd you find the money?"

"Deductive reasoning, I guess, Coy."

"Now who's being the smartass?"

"I just looked around. It happened more by accident than anything."

"Why'd you decide to look for it anyway?"

"'Cause they said they were rolling wheelbarrows full of money outta the church. Said they actually have deacons carrying guns in front of God and everybody to protect it."

"So you thought we ought to come here and steal money from God?"

"Coy, we ain't stealing money from God."

"We're stealing from His church."

"You know as well as I do that ain't no real church."

"How come it ain't?"

Marshall rolled his eyes like I was too smart to act this dumb, but I wasn't playing. I didn't know anything about this church. Other than they'd moved into town a few months ago and were meeting in what used to be a convenience store.

"C'mon, Coy, they do all that dancing and shouting and praying for healing. The preacher parades around, carrying rattlesnakes in one hand and a bottle of olive oil in the other. Talks about casting out devils and speaking in tongues."

"It ain't the first church like that in Tugalo County."

"Yeah, but them other preachers got a little modesty to 'em. They drive a used truck instead of something brand new with all the tricks."

"Where's this church getting all this money then, Marshall? It ain't like the other holy rollers ever hauled around wheelbarrows full of cash."

"Hell, if I know. I was just thinking they wouldn't never know it if we took a share."

"Why didn't you take some when you first found the cash?"

"I did. Took a couple hundred bucks to make sure it would spend. Went to the store, and the girl used one of them markers to make sure it was real. When she didn't say nothing, I brought you here for us to get as much as we could."

"That didn't work out too good, did it, little brother?"

"Sure as hell didn't. How you think we can get outta here?"

That was something I needed to think about. It wasn't that there were a lot of options to consider. Most of them ended with us getting shot, and I liked my body not having no bullet holes in it. What little time there was for me to think was ticking away fast. Andy would get back with her Deddy any time now. That told me what we needed to do, but Marshall wasn't going to like it no more than I did.

"What?" Marshall asked.

"You ain't gone like this one bit."

"Can't know if you don't tell me."

"I think we should go with the flow."

"You're right. I don't like it."

"Well hell, Marshall, you're the one that asked. If you got any better suggestions, let's hear 'em."

Marshall took a deep breath like his brain needed the extra oxygen for thinking and started to answer, but Harper Lewellen interrupted him. "All right, boys, I'm opening this here door, and if y'all do anything stupid, I'm sending you both right to Hell, understand me?"

5.

Harper Lewellen stood at the lip of the hole wearing his house slippers, a wrinkled pair of sweatpants, but no shirt. The man looked like an aging mastiff with slack jowls and a triple-layer chin. All the muscles he'd built were getting worn out and replaced with flab. His eyes were still crusty with sleep and his hair a mess. Andy was fully clothed now but looked good as ever. She moved away from the side of her Deddy. They both aimed shotguns at us.

"Mack Dooley," Harp said my name like he'd bitten into a persimmon and made a face to go along with it, "you remember what I said I'd do if I ever saw your face again?"

"Yessir, sure do," I looked around the barrel that Harper aimed in my face and up into his crusty eyes, "and I was just thinking at least these're better circumstances to have to shoot me under."

Andy blushed, and Harp snorted. Marshall muttered something which got Harp's attention, and he said, "What'd you say, boy?"

Marshall said, "I was trying to tell my brother to keep his goddamn mouth shut before we end up having to pick buckshot from each other's asses."

If Harper thought of shooting me first, his mind changed by the time Marshall figured it was best to zip his lips. The shotgun swung in my brother's direction, and the sleepy look turned to a thunder cloud. He spoke with a bone-white grip on his gun, "You better listen to me right now, boy, we don't take the Lord's name in vain in this house, and if I hear you use it like that one more time I'll blow your head right off your shoulders. Hear me?"

Marshall got stiff all over, but he kept a cool gaze on Harp. I didn't know if he was going to answer him at first, but when Marshall spoke it was with an even tone. "Pardon my language, Lew. Won't happen again."

Harper eased his grip on his gun and said, "Let's get another thing straight. I ain't the same man y'all's Deddy used to run with when y'all was little. The Lord's done a lot to change me and I'd rather y'all not call me by none of the names your Deddy did. Just Harper or Brother Harper. Any other name than them, and I'll give this trigger finger of mine a scratch."

"All right, Harper," I said, taking the lead, "what do we need to do to get you to let us outta this hole?"

He balanced the shotgun's barrel on his shoulder and let it point at the roof of the building. "Letting y'all outta this hole ain't up to me, boys. Andrea here called Preacher Randy after she woke me up, and he's on his way over. He's the one who hears from the Lord, and by the time he gets here he'll let us know what to do with you."

"Wait a minute, Harp—"

"Hey, what'd I tell you about calling me by the names of my Old Man? He's dead. According to God's Word,

I'm a New Man. A New Creature, Mack. It says that in Second Corinthians 5:17. *'Old things have passed away, and all things have become new.'*"

I held my hands up to let Harper know I was wrong and apologized. I didn't know anything about this Preacher Randy and didn't want to try my luck with somebody who let his deacons carry. Our chances were better with Harper, and I let him know it. "All I was going to say is there ain't no reason to bring the preacher into this. It's your land we was trespassing on. Might as well be you that decides what to do with us."

I looked over at Marshall and could tell by the look on his face I ought to be speaking Geechee, but he went along with me. "Mack's right," he said, "why wait up all night on a preacher that'll probably turn us loose?"

My brother wasn't joking, but Harper laughed like hell, the sound of it ricocheting off the building's aluminum walls. Andy spoke over him and said, "Deddy, I think they're scared of dealing with Brother Randy."

"Sure does sound that way, doesn't it?" Harp's cheeks turned red from a smile that stretched his lank jowls, and he used the back of a hairy arm to wipe tears from his eyes. "Y'all got the wrong idea about Brother Jessup. He ain't some soft-hearted preacher that'll just turn you loose. He'll pray in earnest about it, and if the Lord tells him to deal y'all justice, he will."

Harper let the last word hang in the air until it faded away and made for the door. "We'll give y'all some time to get right with God. Preacher'll be here soon."

6.

Unless God decided to show up and free us from this hole the way He freed Daniel from the lion's den, then it'd be a waste of time for us to get right with Him. We tried busting the door off its lock. Marshall gave me a boost, and I slammed my shoulder into it. It rattled on its hinges, but it didn't budge. After three tries total, I walked away dizzier than a quarterback hit from his blindside and massaged my shoulder.

Marshall waited for me to stop babying myself and then told me to do the same with him. With the way my shoulder ached, I didn't have the strength to lift him, and he wasn't no more of a battering ram than me, so I told him no. He looked at the door like he might be able to stare a hole through it and asked, "What're we gone do then?"

"I don't know," I said. "But I don't like the idea of going with the flow no more."

"Damn if I don't either." Marshall walked over to the shelves and grabbed one of the cans. "What if we started hurling these sumbitches at 'em whenever they lift the door?"

"You gone throw that can at 'em hard enough to

knock 'em out?"

"Probably not. It could create a distraction though."

"It could. But they'd just end up shooting us."

Marshall sat the can down like he discovered an ancient curse was connected to it and walked over to the money. He started taking it by the handful and stuffing it into his pockets.

"What the hell're you doing?" I asked.

He stopped and looked at me, said, "This's what I came down here for, and I'm at least gone leave with a little bit of it."

"You know they ain't gone let you keep it."

Marshall's front pockets bulged now, and he stuffed bills into his back pockets. "I'm fully aware of that. But if they spend all their time searching me for money, they might forget why they're here in the first place."

"That's why they're here, Marshall."

Marshall swatted away my words the way he did when a gnat dive-bombed around his head, "You had your idea. Now I have mine."

It didn't make any sense to me—but I figured it'd slow them down if there were two of us to search, so I joined my brother at the cabinets. He'd filled his back pockets and unbuckled his belt to stuff cash down the legs of his jeans.

"Maybe they'll forget some of it, and we'll make out with a little bit of cash anyway."

"If we even get outta this alive."

"You think that preacher'll kill us?"

His question stopped me from stuffing my pockets. "I don't know nothing 'bout this preacher, but I don't like the way old Harp was talking 'bout him."

"You see the way Andy's eyes started twinkling when her deddy brought him up?"

I filled my pockets, undid my belt, and stuffed the legs of my jeans with cash. "Saw that," I said, "she always got that look on her face when we messed around."

"Wait a minute," Marshall stopped me, "you're telling me Andy's sleeping with the preacher?"

"If she ain't sleeping with him, then she's thinking 'bout it."

"Good God."

"You're surprised?" I asked. "Look at all this money, Marshall. This seem like something honest a preacher'd be into? I bet Andy's not the only girl in the church he's sleeping with either."

Marshall turned his attention to the door. We heard voices outside, and one carried over all the rest. The person spoke with a musical quality making their voice ring as if a large crowd clung to every word. I guessed it was Randy Jessup. Only preachers and politicians speak that way regardless of how many ears are listening. He made a joke which got everybody laughing and then told them to open the door.

Marshall cinched his belt tight, left the cabinets for the door, and said, "Let's raise hell, Coy."

7.

I didn't have no idea what my brother planned. Following each other's lead had us in a situation where we'd hopped from one damn hole to another. I nodded at Marshall and tightened my belt around my waist.

Marshall walked to the front of the storm shelter, and when they opened the door, a tall man looked down on him. The man wore a black suit that fit tight like it'd got bought with someone else's money. He carried a black Bible with worn leather and faded golden-edged pages. An eye patch covered his left eye with a snow-white dove printed on the front of it. His mouth curled back into a snarl and his good eye danced between the two of us. A pair of big men bookended the preacher. I recognized the brothers from high school but hadn't kept up with either since.

They ran in the same group as Andy and me and were a couple of cans short of a six-pack. If they were with the preacher, it didn't mean anything good for us. They'd spent more time suspended from school for fighting than in the classroom.

Marshall put his hands out to the side like he was

inviting the preacher in for a hug and said, "Brother Jessup, sure is good to see you here."

The preacher's one eye flicked over to my brother, and when he spoke in that sing-song tone, he asked, "Excuse me, friend, but do I know you?"

Marshall dropped his hands back to his sides, and they thumped against the money stuffed into his pants pockets. "You mean our buddy Harper there didn't make you aware of who we are?"

Harper stood off to the side with Andy. They both still carried their shotguns and looked a little concerned about Marshall's question. The preacher turned to them and then back to my brother. That snarl still curled his upper lip. He said, "I asked Brother Harper not to influence my thoughts about y'all boys. That way, when the Lord speaks to me, I'll hear him clearly."

"That's much appreciated then," Marshall said. "Old Lew ain't got shit good to say 'bout my brother back there."

"Hey," Harper started but stopped when the preacher turned to him.

"Don't fret, Brother Harper, a man of the world, will use the language of the world. It does not influence me one bit."

The preacher leaned down on a knee and looked towards the back of the shelter where I was. It felt like he was trying to use that one good eye to poke around inside my head, and I focused my thoughts on keeping him out of there.

"What terrible things could Brother Harper have to say about your brother?"

Marshall laughed. "One time, my brother and his daughter over there wore out some shock absorbers in the back of one of his cars. Told him if he saw them like that again, he'd blow his damn head off."

The preacher's eyebrows raised at that, and he turned to look at Andy. Her cheeks burned like she caught a fever, and she couldn't look him in the eye. He turned back to Marshall and said, "Friend, the Word of God says in the book of Isaiah that God blots out our transgressions for His own sake and does not remember our sins."

"Well, preacher, I can tell you my brother remembers every sin he committed with Andrea Lewellen clear as yesterday."

The preacher's snarl became a scowl, and he stood. He dusted dirt from the knee of his pants leg and looked down at the two of us. He didn't speak for a long time. All anybody could hear was the breathing in the room. Once he sorted through his thoughts, he turned to his men and said, "Get them outta that hole."

8.

The Eli brothers were both built like a pair of feral hogs. They were hard round men who were all shoulders and no neck. They'd knock the hell out of anybody who got in their way. Their fists balled when the preacher told them to help us out of the hole, hoping for a fight. I started having doubts about following Marshall's lead, but this all seemed part of his plan. He threw his hands back up and said, "Whoa there, preacher! You ain't gotta sic them boys on us. We'll come out willingly."

Cody and Cory both stopped. My brother's claim confused them, and they looked back at the preacher. Randy Jessup grasped his Bible tight in both hands like the power of its words would bleed from the pages into him. I thought my brother might have the preacher stressed out a little bit, and he tried not to show it. He closed his eye to think - and then opened it. "If the Lord is moving on his heart to come out of that hole willingly, then let him come. Just keep a close eye on him and make sure he don't try nothing funny."

"Now, preacher, if the Lord is moving on my heart - why would you think I would try anything funny?"

Randy Jessup kneaded his fingers into the Bible like a baker molding a piece of dough and gave Marshall a long look with his one eye. He dropped his tone close to a whisper, and I strained to hear what he said, "Friend, the book of Jeremiah says the heart is deceitful above all things and is desperately wicked. The Lord might move on our heart, but we are still sinful beings who want to fulfill the desires of our flesh."

"Well, if it makes you feel any better," Marshall said, "I'll swear before God to do exactly what He tells me."

Randy Jessup darkened the hole and leaned in. "Brother, don't go and swear before the Lord if you're not planning on keeping your word."

The preacher couldn't figure out if Marshall meant to test him like the children of Israel did the Lord while journeying through the wilderness. The whole fiasco made the Eli brothers antsy. I'd bet the hundred-dollar bills stuffed under my crotch if my brother kept giving him lip - he'd unleash the Elis and let them fulfill their violent fantasies.

Marshall stood up straight and put a hand over his heart. "I do so solemnly swear that whenever God moves on my heart, I will do what he tells me without a second thought. In the name of Jesus, I pray," Marshall paused, "or whatever this is I'm doing. Amen."

The whole room stopped moving, and we waited to see if Randy Jessup would approve of my brother's prayer. The Bible hung loose in his hands now, and he glared at my brother through a narrow eyelid.

When he didn't speak, Marshall said, "How 'bout that, preacher?"

Randy Jessup cleared his throat and drummed his fingers on his Bible. After some thought, he said, "I felt the Lord in that, brother. Amen. Let me back my boys up here. Give y'all some room to crawl outta that hole."

Marshall turned to me once the preacher got the Eli brothers to back off some, and he shot me the smile which led us into all this trouble.

I knew he was about to break his promise to God.

"Hey, Coy," Marshall whispered, "you remember that time at the football game where Coach put me in to kick that game-winning field goal against Blackwood?"

"Coach never put you in to kick no field goals, Marshall," I said, "What the hell you talking about right now?"

"Sure he did." He shrugged. "The Lord just reminded me of it."

Randy Jessup walked up to the edge of the hole and said, "What're y'all boys talking about?"

"We're just trying to decide who's coming outta this hole first," Marshall said.

Randy Jessup didn't hesitate. "If the Lord is moving on your heart, friend, shouldn't it be you?"

Marshall nodded. "You're right, preacher. I just needed to hear it from a man of God."

Randy Jessup stepped back and gave my brother plenty of room to boost himself out of the hole. Marshall took his time approaching the edge, and before he lifted himself out, he turned to me. "Don't forget how I kicked that field goal, Coy. It won the football game."

I nodded to my brother without a word, and he grabbed onto the ledge. Once he started lifting himself out of the hole, I walked up behind him and held my hand out to the preacher. "Say, preacher, you mind giving me a hand outta here? Got a bad shoulder."

When the preacher grabbed my hand, I locked the

other over his wrist the way a professional wrestler sets his opponent up for a devastating finisher. Marshall reared back and kicked Cory Eli in the ball sack like he meant for the pigskin to sail fifty-five yards for a game clincher. Before Randy Jessup could turn and see why Cory hollered, I gave his arm a jerk.

9.

There was nothing graceful in the way the preacher fell. He somersaulted ass over elbows and hit the concrete floor with the kind of thump that hurts everybody watching. I kicked him in the mouth before he could get himself together. His head snapped to the side, and a red streak smeared across the floor. Andy aimed her shotgun at me and yelled, "Don't you hurt him again!"

I yanked Randy Jessup from the floor so I could play peek-a-boo with the buckshot.

"You let Brother Randy go right now, Mackenzie." Andy knew my mama is the only person I let call me by my full name, and she only did so when she was mad enough to drown puppies.

"Put the gun down, Andy, or I'll make sure Brother Jessup meets God with a hole in his chest."

Andy wasn't sure what to do but couldn't take her eyes away from whatever commotion Marshall caused. The side-by-side shotgun barrels dropped, and she blurted out, "Don't, Deddy, don't."

Harper grunted and fell into the hole next to me. Marshall stood around the corner from Andy and aimed

Harper's shotgun at her head. "Put that gun down, Andy. I ain't never cared for you like my brother did. Won't bother me none to shoot you."

Andy's brain popped like the time I dared Marshall to stick a fork in the power socket. She aimed the gun all around like she was scribbling signals in the air, looking back and forth between Randy Jessup and my brother. Marshall wasn't lying about blowing her head off, and I was about to have to tell her again to put the gun down, but the preacher cut me off like he was the only one she'd listen to.

"Sister Andrea," he cleared his throat and spit blood at my feet, "put the gun down like he's telling you to. They won't hurt us no worse than they already have. The Lord's spoken to me."

"You must not have been tuned in to the Lord too good if you didn't see none of this coming, huh, preacher?" Marshall asked.

"Second Corinthians tell us Satan can transform himself into an angel of light, brother," Randy Jessup answered, "but don't you worry. Vengeance belongs to the Lord, and He will have his justice."

Andy aimed the shotgun at Marshall once the Eli brothers came back down to earth and stood with all the speed of a blowup doll. Marshall said, "Andy, I'm giving you 'til the count of three to put that fucking gun down, or I'm gone shoot your deddy along with everybody else in here."

Andy dropped to a knee and sat her gun on the concrete before my brother could even start his countdown. She backed away from it without being told to, too. Instead, she held her hands high and turned on the tears.

Marshall gave her his back and aimed his gun at the

Elis. "Coy, grab that gun and get outta that hole. Gimme some backup up here."

I knocked the preacher to his knees, kicked him in the back, and commanded him to lay flat on his belly. He turned his head to glare at me with his one working eyeball. Its pale blue flame almost stopped me in my tracks, but I stepped over him and did like my brother asked, and grabbed the shotgun, and swung it in the direction of the Eli brothers.

They'd never seen an obstacle they couldn't muscle their way through, and I wasn't sure they didn't believe a bullet wouldn't slow them down.

Marshall said, "Get y'all's big asses down in that hole 'fore I put a bullet clear through both of you."

The Elis weren't used to being threatened. They didn't do what Marshall told them. Instead, they stood there and dared him to pull the trigger. If the first bullet didn't take them down, they'd be coming after us. But the preacher butted in again.

"Boys," he said, "don't test this man's willingness to do what he says. We already know he won't hesitate to break his word to the Lord. He is capable of all sorts of evil. Don't be a victim of him. Let the Lord deal with him."

Without question, the Eli brothers moved toward the hole, and we got out of their way so they could hop down inside. Cory helped the preacher stand and Cody checked on Old Harp.

Andy was the only one who was left. When Marshall raised his shotgun at her, I put my hand on the barrel.

"What the hell?" He said.

"You ain't gotta aim that gun at her. She'll get down in that hole without you doing that. Ain't that right,

Andy?" She'd already been traumatized enough, and I felt sorry for her.

Without answering my question, she walked over to the hole and the preacher's outstretched hands. Once she took her place next to him, he turned to us and said, "The Lord saw fit to take my eye from me when I was overseas fighting for my country in Afghanistan. He did that so I would lean on him and rely on my spiritual sight. Y'all can't understand the kinda gift that was. The Lord shows me all kinds of things. And right now, He's showing me the kinda vengeance He's going to take on y'all."

Before the preacher could describe that vengeance, Marshall walked over to the door and kicked one of the hinges. It fell shut on Randy Jessup's words, and I slid the lock through its loop.

"Coy, let's get outta here before the Lord lights that crackpot sumbitch up with fire from Heaven."

10.

Outside, Marshall shot out the off-roading tires on the preacher's charcoal F-150, whooping along to the echo of the shotgun blasts when they came back to him. I took off through the field on my own, but it wasn't long before Marshall's bootheels kicked through the grass and passed me, trailing one-hundred-dollar bills behind him. It got me so tickled I couldn't run, so I tried to snatch up as many of them as I could.

Marshall waited for me at the edge of the tree line. The clouds were scattered now, and the moonlight shined bright enough for me to see the crazy glint in his eye. "You believe all that shit back there? Can't believe we came out alive."

I shoved the money Marshall lost into his hand. "Let's not waste no time standing 'round talking 'bout it. Who knows how long they'll be stuck in that hole."

Marshall stuffed the bills down the front of his jeans. "You think they got anybody that'll come unlock that door for 'em?"

"I figure your shotgun blasts woke somebody else up," I said, "who knows how long it'll take 'em to figure out they're down in that hole, and I don't wanna be here when they do."

Marshall didn't argue with my line of reasoning and jogged to catch up with me. My truck was parked just down the hill from where we'd snuck in the fence, and I didn't waste no time heading to it.

At the fence, I pumped the action on the shotgun until there was a pile of shells at my feet and busted the gun's barrel over a fence post. Marshall did the same, and when he dropped the gun in the grass, I pulled the barbed wire up for him.

Marshall grabbed me by the shoulders on the other side, helping me get back to my feet, and said, "Hey, Coy, we're fucking rich."

The truth was we'd stolen only a few thousand dollars, but it was some of the easiest money we'd ever come by, and it would spend easier than any money we'd earned from an honest day's work. I slapped Marshall on the shoulder. "First round is on me."

"Hell yeah."

We hopped our way down the hill, and when we reached my truck, we jumped inside. I didn't wait for Marshall's door to shut before I had the engine started and shifted into drive. I turned to him and said, "You know we need to take a few days and lay low, right?"

He agreed, and I peeled ass out of there.

PART TWO

Lo! On the water's brink we stand
To do the Father's will
To be baptised by his command
And thus the word fulfil

1.

Me and Marshall ain't never been no good at laying low. We got our Deddy's way of peacocking in us, and over the years, it's got us into more than a truckload of trouble. For instance, one time in high school, I stole the answers to Miss Stanley's Algebra 1 finals. She didn't like my brother and threatened to have him kicked off the Titans if he didn't pass with better than a B+. Instead of keeping my theft a secret, Marshall recognized an economic opportunity because everyone at Tugalo County High School knew Miss Stanley gave the most miserable finals. We sold the answers to each of his classmates for twenty bucks apiece. When the whole class passed with an A, she gave them all ISS until we got ratted out. Coach made us run Oklahoma Drills until we both got carried off the practice field on stretchers.

The first couple of nights after robbing Old Lew, we hid out in our trailer and wondered if any of the cars driving by looked suspicious. We watched the news to make sure there wasn't any stories on there about Harp's place getting held up or that we might be at large. Around the second or third night, we started getting stir crazy.

Marshall stretched out in his recliner, sipping on a Terrapin Rye, and Deddy's favorite gun laid on the arm-rest next to him. I watched a report about UGA's spring practice when Marshall said, "I don't know how much more of this shit I can take, Coy."

"How much more of what shit?"

"This." Marshall kicked the footrest down and motioned around the living room. "All we done since we stole that money is sit around here. We ain't spent none of it. Ain't even gone out and got groceries."

"Marshall, I told you back at Harp's place we'd have to take a few days and lay low. You know that preacher's mad as hell and'll want his money back."

"Don't you think if he was gone try and take it from us, he'd've already done it?" Marshall took a hard swig from his beer so that his Adam's apple bobbed the way a fishing lure does when fish ain't biting and went on. "Andy knows we live here and could've done led the whole church here if she wanted to. She ain't done it yet though."

"You ever think that they might be waiting for us to drop our guard?"

Marshall rocked back in the recliner and drank his beer until the can crunched in his hand and dropped it in a growing pile beside his chair. "It's been three days, Coy. I need to get out into the world for my own sanity. Have a drink together at a bar and talk to some girls. I'm tired of looking at your face."

Marshall was right. I was tired of sitting around with nothing else to look at but him. I loved my brother, but he wasn't close to being as pretty as some of the girls I knew. We needed a night out to raise some hell. If for no other reason than to keep us from arguing.

There's nothing more boring than sitting around waiting for something bad to happen.

"Where you wanna go?" I asked.

Marshall whooped and slung himself out of the recliner towards his bedroom and spoke over his shoulder as he went, "Figured Blackwood, and hit the Due South. I was talking with Brystal earlier, and she said she'd be there with some of her friends."

"When the hell were you talking with Brystal?"

He stopped. "She called me when you were taking a nap."

"We're supposed to have our phones turned off, Marshall."

"It was just a quick call, Coy."

I sat on the couch while Marshall got ready. There wasn't no way of knowing if he'd told Brystal about the money. We'd have more than just the preacher and his church after us if he did.

"What the hell're you doing, Coy?"

"Thinking."

"'Bout what? You need to get ready."

If I asked Marshall what I wanted to ask him, the chances of him lying to me were better than average, but I asked him anyway. "Did you tell Brystal about the money?"

"Goddamn, Coy, do you think I'm that damn dumb?"

"You been hiding from me that you been talking to her, Marshall."

"Only 'cause I knew you'd act like this right here." Marshall pointed his finger at me. "But that don't mean I'm fixing to go and talk about the money. Deddy taught me all the same lessons he taught you."

Marshall was referring to our Deddy's number one

rule about living a life of crime, don't talk to nobody about the things you do because you don't never know who you can trust. I wanted to ask Marshall how it worked out for Deddy since he'd got locked up in Sweetwater State Penitentiary ever since we were little. All the good it would've done is piss him off because Marshall got sensitive where our Deddy is concerned.

Instead, I asked, "You even know who all's coming out tonight?"

"You wanna know if Charlene's gone be there?"

"Maybe," I said. "It'll put me in a better mood if she is."

2.

harlene wasn't with Brystal and her friends. Her ex-boyfriend got back from a long haul, and she went to hear Blackberry Smoke with him in Athens. That left me sitting at the bar by myself while Marshall danced with Brystal - and her friends watched me drink. It wasn't that I didn't think any of them girls were pretty, but I got my heart set on having a dance with Charlene, and I let my blues anchor me to a barstool.

Marshall couldn't have cared less about my down-heartedness. He'd come out for a good time and wasn't nobody stopping him. Hell, if anybody asked him to, Marshall wouldn't have been able to point me out at the bar. He'd hugged up with Brystal real tight, his hands shoved down her back pockets, and she giggled at whatever he said and kissed him on the cheek.

One of the girls who met us here decided I'd sulked long enough, left her barstool, and came over to sit next to me. I couldn't remember her name, but I'd been checking her out all night. She wore cowboy boots and cutoff shorts and had the kind of thighs that could squeeze the life from a man.

She sat close to me at the bar and got my attention

by bumping her hip into mine. I quit peeling the label from my beer bottle, glanced over at her, and she smiled at me the way a bobcat does when it's gnawing on the bones of a bunny.

"You just gonna sit here and pout all night, sweetness?" She asked.

I guess she couldn't remember my name either. "I ain't pouting."

"Yeah, you are, sweetie. You've been sitting there nursing that beer, hoping it'll ruin your brother's good time. Don't know whether you can tell or not, but he ain't paying you no attention."

Instead of taking a sip from my beer, I took a long swig, draining the rest of it in a single drink. Then sat the bottle down with a thump. "Look like I was nursing it then?"

She shook her head and turned on her barstool, and our knees bumped together. Her smile turned hungry on me, and I thought she'd eat me in front of everybody if I didn't say something.

"You'll have to forgive me for forgetting, but what'd you say your name was?"

"Jessa Rae Cash." She put her hand out to me. I took it and noticed the softness of her skin. Jessa let the hold linger. "You remember wrestling against my brother in high school? He wrestled for Blackwood, and you would've gone on to the state finals if he hadn't've beat you."

I let my hand drop to the bar, turning back to my beer. "Guess you came over here to ruin my night?"

Jessa ran her hand across my back and dug her nails into my skin. "C'mon, sweet thing, that was almost ten years ago. There ain't no way you can still be mad about that. Didn't you win state the very next year?"

I turned back to Jessa and gave her my own hungry smile. "You some kinda stalker or something, girl? Sounds like you know as much about me as I know."

Jessa leaned into me, and the front of her shirt fell open. She caught my eyes wandering down there and pinched my arm. When I looked back into her eyes, she spoke right into my face, and her breath smelled like peppermint and cinnamon. "Sweetheart, you ain't famous enough for me to stalk. But I do remember you looking real nice in one of them wrestling singlets. Maybe you'll wanna wear one for me later on tonight?"

I leaned away from her to make sure I wasn't just hearing things and looked deeper into her eyes. Some women will say whatever when they think free drinks are coming their way. A good many girls ditched me after they got a shot or two of Fireball into their system. But if it was the Fireball talking, Jessa was doing a hell of a job of hiding it. She ran her hand up my thigh, digging her nails into the inside of my leg.

"I can't even remember if I've still got my singlet."

"It don't matter if you do, sweetie. I would rather you show me some of your favorite wrestling moves."

3.

Jessa led me out to her car without giving me time to tell Marshall I was leaving. She said he would figure it out whenever he noticed I was gone - and probably wouldn't even miss me. Her hind end wiggled when she walked, making it hard for me to think and easy to bump into her trying to get her door. She grabbed ahold of me when she stumbled back, and I scooped an arm around her hips. Her eyes twinkled in the parking lot light above us, and I leaned in for another kiss. Our tongues did a slippery dance until they found a whirling rhythm, leaving us both breathless when we pulled apart.

She hadn't caught her breath yet when she said, "Hurry up and get my door for me."

She dug around her purse for the keys, and I jerked on the handle, but it was locked. Jessa giggled while I teased her neck with kisses and hugged all over her. When my hands made it down to her hips, she pushed me away.

"You wanna get outta here or not?" She said.

"This's just as good a place as any, ain't it?"

Jessa pinched my arm, and this time it hurt. "I ain't

doing nothing in the parking lot of no hillbilly bar."

I put my hands up in surrender, taking a step away. "I didn't know this was a date."

She looked at me and laughed. "Shit, you didn't even buy me a drink, did you?"

I shrugged. "Hell, I can't remember if I paid for mine."

"We better get outta here then," she said, pulling her key ring from her purse, unlocked the door, and let me open it for her. Jessa tossed her purse into the back, plopped her ass down into the driver's seat, and leaned over the console to unlock the door. Her shorts inched up her thighs and squeezed her ass, slowing the blood flow to my brain so bad I forgot to go get in the car. She turned back to me. "What are you waiting on? Get in the car." After she lifted the enchantment she put me in - I ran around to the other side of the car while she argued with the ignition, making the engine knock when it turned over, and I wondered if we'd make it anywhere.

Jessa pulled me in for a kiss and ran her hand down to my crotch, she squeezed my balls, and I said, "Thought you wasn't gone do nothing in no parking lot?"

"I ain't," she said, "but I'm curious about what I get to play with," she added, without bothering to pull away from our lip lock.

"It'll do what needs doing."

That made her giggle. "Let's go find out then, sweetheart."

She tried to push me over to my side of the car, but I came back over and kissed her neck while she backed out of the spot. "You'll make me wreck if you ain't careful."

"You wanna go back to my place?"

She stomped on the brake when a truck backed into her peripheral vision and looked over at me. It was the first time all night she didn't act a flirt with me. "Not if your brother will be home later on tonight."

"Shit, probably," I said. "Unless he goes home with Brystal, but she usually comes over to our place."

Jessa drove her car to the end of the row and followed the truck to the parking lot's exit. In the glow of the Due South neon bar sign, her smile stretched clear across her face and exposed all her teeth, reminding me of a lioness who kills the antelope for her pride. The only thing missing was a stain of blood around her mouth. "I know somewhere we can go."

"Where to?"

"You'll see." She let the next car go by before she turned out into traffic towards the highway. She pointed her hood ornament towards Tugalo County, making me wonder where she could be taking us. She didn't let me get too deep into thought about it because a hand reached over and made its way between my legs and caressed my crotch. I took my eyes off the road to make sure she watched where she was going. It was hard to care too much because the way she touched me made me squirm.

"I couldn't stop thinking about how good you felt earlier."

"It's gone feel even better here in a few minutes."

She squeezed me again hard enough to make me yelp. I damn near stood up in my seat, and she said, "Sorry, sweetie, you got me too excited."

I looked back at the road and saw we were heading toward downtown. I asked, "Where is it you're taking me?"

She worked her hand faster, and it made me want to melt right there in the seat, but she stopped and turned the steering wheel hand over hand. That's when I saw the thick crimson letters painted on the plywood sign that read, LAST WAVE REVIVAL CENTER. Under that, in smaller black letters, it read, HERE WE HAVE SIGNS WONDERS AND MIRACLES FROM GOD!!!

Before I could ask why the hell she brought us here, the truck from the bar pulled in behind us with its brights washing out the dusk in the cab of her car.

4.

My body slammed onto the concrete. Any fight left in me went with the breath forced from my lungs. Two giants jerked me off the ground and tossed me into the side of Jessa's car, and gravity took over. A bootheel stomped my back twisting back and forth, grinding me into the pavement, leaving me feeling like a smashed bug.

That's when I heard Jessa get out of her car, slam her door, and holler over, "Y'all ain't gotta hurt him too bad. He was nice to me all night."

The defense she made for me didn't matter a damn bit to the men manhandling me. I got shoved back into the side of her car, where Cory and Cody Eli's ugly mugs stared at me confused.

"You brought us the wrong brother."

Jessa's cowboy boots clinked along the pavement when she made her way over to our side of the car. "Excuse me?"

I shoved the Eli brothers while Jessa distracted them, but Cory gut-punched me hard enough I thought I crapped myself. I sat pinned against the car, and Cody grabbed Jessa by the arm. She asked him what the hell he thought he was doing and tried to take her arm back, but he rag-dolled her over and made her look me in the face.

Her expression was no longer grave. She was scared now. Her eyelids blurred like hummingbird wings while her bottom lip quivered, and tears fell.

Cody leaned down next to her face. His lips pulled back, and he showed off a gap-toothed snarl. "You see that you got us the wrong brother now?"

Jessa tried shaking her head, but Cody held her by the hair. "Marshall was with his girlfriend." She cried. "Wouldn't even pay attention to me. There wasn't no way I'd be able to separate him from her."

"Then you knew you brought us the wrong brother?"

Cody slammed her into the side of her car and grabbed her throat. Her voice strained when she spoke. "What else did you want me to do? I couldn't just start a fight with Brystal in the middle of the bar. Marshall would've been on her side. Thought the next best plan was for me to bring y'all Mack. If he don't know what y'all want y'all can use him to trap Marshall."

Neither of the Eli brothers argued with Jessa. "Can y'all let me go now? I did the best I could and at least got y'all one of the Dooley brothers. It won't be hard for y'all to get the other one."

"We'll have to clear it with Brother Jessup first. He's the one who specified which Dooley to bring us." Cory jerked me off the ground and wrenched one of my arms behind my back. It brought me up to my tiptoes, and he led me toward the church entrance.

"Hey," Jessa said, and I could hear her trying to get away from Cody, "I'll give y'all back the money y'all gave me. I ain't even spent none of it yet. Just don't make me go see that preacher."

Cory stopped me at the church doors. A faint glow came from the sanctuary, and a big cross made a shadow over the room. We waited for Cody to bring Jessa, but he struggled to get a hold of her. She kicked and clawed, and when he had enough of that, he let a backhand across her face that dropped her to the pavement. She fell in a heap by her car, and he scooped her up like a sack of groceries.

"You got the keys?" Cody asked.

Cory said, "Ain't you got 'em?"

"You leave 'em in the truck?" Cody nodded over at it.

Cory said, "I ain't had 'em on me."

"What the hell, Cory?"

"Just knock on the damn door."

"Don't let him hear you talk like that."

Cory got stiff when his language got mentioned and hushed up faster than a Sunday morning altar call. Cody pushed me against a window, so my face smushed against it, banged on the door, rattling the whole frame.

Randy Jessup moved like a silhouette in the dark. He'd rolled his shirt sleeves to the elbows and changed into khakis instead of funeral black. He approached the door without his eyepatch on to hide the thick scar tissue where an eye should've been. He took in the scene outside with his good eye and unlocked the door.

5.

I fell at the preacher's feet. He took a step back and out of the way when I got pulled to my feet. The Lord must have been whispering to him in His still small voice because that's when I whirled around with a hard right, knocking the spit out of Cody's mouth and making him stumble drunkenly, shoving him back into his brother. Cory dropped Jessa on the floor. She let out a cry when she hit the tiles, but it went ignored. Both brothers came after me, but things went differently than any of us were planning. Cody wrestled me around while Cory threw wild punches and knocked the hell out of us both. There wasn't no getting away for me, but I thought my fighting could help Jessa flee. The preacher made sure it didn't happen.

"Y'all are letting the girl get away."

Cory turned to see Randy Jessup pointing toward the door, and it put me one-on-one with Cody again. Blood drizzled from where I'd lacerated his lip with the stone in my state championship ring. He brought his fists up to his face and swayed like a punch dizzied boxer, but before we could go at it, the preacher stepped between us with arms outstretched the way a referee does when making a stoppage.

"Listen, friend," the preacher said, "you can try and fight all you want, but all you'll do is make it worse for the lady. She's got punishment coming her way for not bringing me your brother. Do you really want her carrying your share of judgment?"

I dropped my fists. "What kinda fucking preacher are you?"

Randy Jessup folded his arms in front of his chest and took a step closer to me. He must have thought crowding up on me like that would intimidate me, but I took a step forward. We were close enough to smell each other's breath, and I could see Cody getting ready to pounce in case the preacher needed help.

Randy Jessup used his preaching voice when he spoke, and it boomed around the church's foyer. "Friend, I would ask you to refrain from using foul language in the house of the Lord. Speak however you'd like out in the world but show this place some respect."

In the sorts of situations, my mama always said to keep my mouth shut. But too much of my deddy got mixed into the ingredients when they made me. "This used to be a goddamn Dixie Mart, you crooked ass preacher."

A flood of fury filled the preacher's eye, and I braced myself for the wrath of God, but right then, Cory brought Jessa inside for her come-to-Jesus meeting. The girl raised hell and Randy Jessup turned away from me to watch her pitch an ungodly fit. Cody paid no attention to Jessa - instead, he dared me to sucker punch the preacher.

Randy walked over to where Jessa was pinned on the floor and knelt beside her. He ran his fingers through her hair, and I thought it'd make her scream, but she calmed down, confused at his gentle hand. Tears streamed, and she whimpered like a kicked dog, but she stopped all that to listen to what the preacher had to say.

"Sister Jessa, it's doing you no favors to lash out this way. It says in Proverbs chapter fifteen, the eyes of the Lord are in every place, beholding the evil and the good. Cut out all this silliness and do not act evil in His sight."

Jessa used the back of her arm to wipe the snot from her nose, and she spoke in between sobs. "I didn't bring you the wrong Dooley on purpose, Brother Jessup. The other one was with his girlfriend, and I didn't know how to get him away from her. I thought I was doing the right thing."

Randy Jessup stood, loomed over Jessa, and placed both hands on his hips. "Proverbs fourteen teaches us that there is a way that seems right to a man," he said, "but the end thereof are the ways of death."

Her voice went up in pitch. "Am I gonna die?"

I lunged forward, but Cody Eli bearhugged me around the shoulders and wrestled me to the wall. A paint-by-numbers scene of Jesus helping Peter walk on water rattled on its hook and crashed on the floor.

Cory stood to help his brother, but Randy Jessup held a hand out. "Stop that foolishness right now, friend, or Sister Jessa will suffer the wrath due you."

6.

Cody bearhugged my arms to my ribs and made it so I couldn't fight. He cradled me the way a mama does a rowdy child and tossed me onto one of the pews when we got into the sanctuary. He pinned me to the seatback. Cory led Jessa down the aisle where Randy Jessup waited. He tossed her at the preacher's feet when they reached the altar. Jessa rolled across the floor, stopping just shy of Randy. He knelt down beside her right after she pushed up onto an elbow, and he helped her stand. Her hair was matted to one side of her face now. Her makeup looked a mess, and her shorts ran up her butt. Randy massaged one of her shoulders and pulled her close.

He embraced her the way an angry parent hugs a frightened child and started praying, "Father God, this wretched soul comes before you unworthy and sinful. She's disobeyed your solemn servant and is here to face Your judgment." Randy Jessup let his voice hitch and turned his face heavenward. "Give her Your strength and help her to stand on her faith and be merciful if You will, Lord. Most of all, be just. As the book of Romans says, for we all have sinned, and come short of the glory of God. In the name of Jesus we pray. Amen."

Randy Jessup held Jessa out at arm's length, and she shook all over. He looked at her with that twinkling eye of his and asked, "What do we say, Sister Jessa?"

She tripped over her tongue when she tried forming words. The preacher asked her the question again, and she forced herself to say an amen.

Randy Jessup motioned Cory over with a Cadillac grin. He turned Jessa so she could see him bring a pine-wood box over with a chicken wire door on top. She almost fell from her feet when she saw - but Randy helped her stand. Cory sat it on the ground in front of them, and the preacher pushed Jessa to her knees. She went slow and cried once her knees knocked against the floor. Cory shook the box around to stir up whatever was inside, unlatched the chicken wire door, and let it spring open.

"What the hell's going on here?" I asked.

Cody dug his fingers into my shoulders, and the preacher turned to us. He said, "You will keep your mouth shut while Sister Jessa is judged by the Lord. If you refuse to do so, I'll allow Cory to do what he sees fit."

Jessa wailed at the threat and balled up on the floor. She held her hands over her head. Cory looked down at her and then at the preacher. He didn't have to say a word because his body language did the talking. He'd already thought of everything he wanted to do with Jessa.

Randy Jessup waited to see if I'd speak, but I didn't open my mouth. He reached down to Jessa and put a hand on her shoulder. She shrugged away from him, and he grabbed her arm and said, "Don't make this worse than it has to be, Sister Jessa. I will force your hand in that box."

Jessa turned to the preacher, and all the fear drained from her face. It left her cheeks colorless and her eyes blank. She knew she couldn't put her hand in that box. Randy Jessup fell backward when Jessa lunged at him. He tried pushing her away, but she was too quick for him. She dug her nails into his face and tried tearing the skin. Cory leaped over the box to help Randy. I tried ejecting myself from the pew, but Cody wrestled me over the back of the seat with a surprise headlock from behind.

He threw me down into the aisle and pinned me to the floor with a knee between my shoulder blades. Cody grabbed my hair and pulled my head back. Cory pulled Jessa off Randy Jessup and tossed her onto the altar. She skidded ass-first down the steps, wailing like a child all the way. The preacher came off the floor and shoved Cody. His greased back hair stood in a cockeyed mohawk with bloodied scratches swelled out on either side of his face. He snarled at Jessa like he wanted to cuss her out.

"Sister Jessa, you've heard me preach from the book of First Chronicles where God says, *'touch not My anointed and do My prophets no harm.'* Do you not recognize my office in His kingdom?" He wiped a hand over his face and smeared bloody streaks across it. Randy bent at the waist and said to her, "The Spirit of Jezebel's done got ahold of you, girl. I now see why the Lord led me to use you to bring this Dooley to me. I was starting to fear I'd misheard Him. It was the Lord's desire to expose your wicked heart. Get your hand in that box."

Jessa leaned as far back on her elbows as she could

to keep away from the preacher. Gooseflesh prickled all over her arms and thighs, and she gnawed into her bottom lip. Randy Jessup leaned in further and spit when he said, "Get up. Get up. Now!"

She fell forward onto her knees. Her hair fell into her face, she didn't take her eyes from the floor, and I knew she'd given up. Randy Jessup reached down, took her by a wrist over to the box.

"I will not say another prayer for you. It's shameful the way you disregarded the other one and exposed your ungrateful heart."

Jessa didn't move. I don't know if she could. Her hand stayed glued to the top of the pinewood, and even when the preacher shouted for Cory to make her obey, she didn't lift a finger. "Don't touch me!" Jessa turned her face up to the preacher and said, "I can't wait to see you in Hell."

He opened his mouth to speak, but she shoved her hand through the top of the pinewood and waited for something to happen, but nothing did. Jessa started laughing. "Was you expecting something more to happen here, Brother Jessup? Looks like the Lord's on my side."

Randy Jessup struck like lightning and shoved Jessa's arm into the box until her shoulder scratched against the splinters. "Remember the book of Galatians, Sister Jessa? God is not one to be mocked. His Word says you will reap what you sow."

Jessa tried pulling her arm from the box, but the preacher pinned her to it. Then he grabbed it by a corner and started shaking it. The box collided against the floor, and Jessa screamed over the racket. He rattled the box harder and harder until it seemed like it'd bust.

Then he stopped. He wrenched Jessa's arm out of the trap and held it to the light, searched it all over until he didn't find what he was looking for, and he pushed her away.

Jessa fell to her side and cradled her arm to her chest. She breathed in heavy sighs. The preacher said, "It looks as if the Lord decided to spare you, Sister Jessa. Do not let this show of mercy be for naught. Continue to serve the Lord just as you have and be available when I call, understand?"

Randy Jessup smoothed the wrinkles from his khakis when he stood. "Help Sister Jessa to her car, Brother Cory, and come right back. We still have our friend here to attend to."

7.

andy Jessup sat in the middle step of the altar and stared at me until Cory found his way back into the sanctuary. The preacher motioned for him to come to the front of the room, and the floorboards balked when he walked by. Once Cory reached the front of the church, Randy had him hand him the three-foot cottonmouth from inside the box. The black and saddle tan bands of the snake glittered in the dingy light of the sanctuary when Cory passed it to the preacher.

Randy Jessup took it in his arms and held its head away from his body. Its tongue flicked out intermittently, and its body laid limp in Randy's lap. He moved his hands toward its head in slow motion, and when they reached its base, they twisted around it. The preacher pulled on the cottonmouth's head, and its body writhed around. He disregarded the way the snake hissed and squeezed until the head popped off clean. The body flexed and coiled and flopped down onto the floor when Randy Jessup stood.

He dropped the head into the pinewood box and told Cory to get rid of the carcass. He walked down the aisle and looked down at me. The preacher told Cody to let me up from the floor. He wanted to speak to me face to face.

My back crackled when he pulled his knee from between my shoulder blades. I rolled over and used the pew next to me to stand.

Randy Jessup asked me to sit and shrugged when I didn't. Cody stepped forward to force me but stopped when the preacher said, "If he'd like to stand, that's okay, Brother Cody. The Lord spoke to me while I took the life from that cottonmouth and said he wouldn't fight." Randy Jessup paused, turned to me, and asked, "What did you think of that?"

"Looks to me like a weak man likes to prey on things that ain't got no more sense than to trust him. Like a woman that's scared to death of him."

Randy Jessup's mouth made a hard line across his face. His eye wandered over the paintings of Jesus hanging from the sanctuary walls, each depicting a different scene from his life. The preacher's hands shoved into his pockets, and he said, "If Sister Jessa has any fear of me, it's not because I've preyed on her. It's because of how the Lord's used me. Not all of His children receive His word joyfully. Some react in fear, others in anger, and still others react in sadness and repentance. Have you never read the Parable of the Sower, friend?"

"Parable of the who?" I asked. "That some kinda riddle?"

"Brother Dooley," the preacher drug out my last name like it was stuck to his tongue, "Jesus taught in stories that we call parables. One of the most famous parables is from the Gospel of Matthew. It's about a sower sowing seed. This sower spreads his seed in all kinds of different ground. Some seed falls where there's no soil, some falls on rocky ground, some of the ground is filled with thorns, and some of it is good. The soil represents a person's heart, and I can tell you right now Sister Jessa's heart is full of thorns."

"Preacher," copying the way he drew my name out, I said, "I think there's a different way to interpret this parable. Sounds to me like you've got this preacher trying to spread his seed among all these gullible women. They all react in different kinds of ways like women are bound to do. But the preacher takes it personal when the woman he's got his good eye set on acts kinda prickly towards him. Maybe he don't plow her garden right or his seed ain't potent. You can't never know when a woman's reasoning is involved."

Randy Jessup's features darkened to the color of an infected pecker sore. "That kinda crudeness will not be tolerated in this house."

A heavy hand laid across the back of my head so hard it made my ankles buckle. I busted my elbows and knees on the tile, and electric pulses emanated from my funny bone. I rolled over onto my ass before anyone could touch me and sat at Cody Eli's feet. The big sonuva bitch looked down at me with a crooked grin and made me laugh.

I looked over at the preacher and said, "You know I went to high school with both the Elis? They were a grade behind me, and we ran with the same group of friends. We didn't never say nothing to their face because we didn't wanna hurt their feelings, but we all thought they were retarded."

Cody's grin fell limp, and his fat jowls drooped with his frown.

"There was this one girl Cody liked, but she wouldn't

never go on a date with him. Don't know if you ever knew why, Cody, but Beth Anne said you didn't have enough brains to get your pecker hard."

Cody roared like a wounded boar and lunged after me but not fast enough. I drop kicked him between the legs. My aim was a little off, and the toe of my boot only grazed his ball sack, but it was enough to send him tumbling into the preacher. They fell into a pew so hard it slid across the floor, banging into the one in front of it, and they fell in a heap.

Cory came back inside before my feet could reach the foyer. My presence startled him - he jerked the door to and twisted the lock. Cody and the preacher fell over each other as they tried to stand. Cory charged forward like a pissed-off defensive lineman, trying to blindside me. I made a rush for the door, but he twirled around on his bootheel and caught me, I stumbled back, tripped over a potted plant, caught myself on a chair, but Cory flipped me over. I hit the floor so hard it took a minute before I realized I wasn't dead.

I looked up to see Randy Jessup standing over me. He clenched his jaw so tight the muscles flexed from the side of his face. "The Lord is the only thing keeping my wrath at bay right now, friend. You've been a thorn in my side from the moment I set eyes on you, and if it were up to me, I'd let the Elis break your bones. The Lord is telling me to reflect on your situation. I'm going to trust in Him, but if you don't change, then I'll beseech the Lord to let me handle you the way I see fit."

Randy Jessup waved a hand and the Elis grabbed me. "Take him to the basement and let him spend the night in the box."

8.

The Elis hauled me to the basement steps like a piece of garbage they meant to toss on a bonfire. When we made it to the door, Cory let go of my legs to twist the knob, and I looked back at Cody and said, "You know what, hoss? Beth Anne never really cared how smart you was. The reason you never got no more than a hand job from her is because she said the only hole on her whole body your pecker was big enough to tease was her belly button."

That was it for Cody. I'd run my mouth so much since the preacher left he couldn't take it no more and took it out on me now. He jerked me by the arms, made me stand, and wrenched an arm around my neck. He twisted the chokehold in tight, and Cory stood there and watched me suffocate. That went on until my vision started getting fuzzy, and all my thoughts got as thin as the air I was breathing. Just before I blacked out, Cory tapped his brother's shoulder, and Cody let me go. I fell at their feet and sucked in all the oxygen my lungs could hold, but the Elis didn't give me long to recover.

Cody grabbed me by the shoulders, tossed me into a wall, and pinned me there. He told Cory to strip me from my clothes, and even though I hadn't caught my breath all the way, I said, "I knew y'all were always a couple of queers. Probably been waiting on this moment since high school. Bet the reason the preacher keeps y'all around is cause y'all let him diddle with your peckers when nobody's looking."

Cody punched the wall beside my head, said, "Stop fucking talking. You don't stop fucking talking - I'll break all your teeth."

Cody whirled me around, smashed my face into the wall until my vision shattered. It was like trying to look through spiderwebbed plate-glass, and my ears started ringing. Cory said, "Keep your cool. Brother Jessup hears you talking like that, and he'll lock you down here with him."

"The girl's down here," Cody said. "I'll show him what kinda queer I am."

Cory grabbed his brother by the front of the shirt. "You won't touch her. You know what he told us."

Cody noticed me trying to slip away from him and slammed me into the wall again. My nose busted. Blood sprayed down my front, and I said, "Goddamn, I think you broke my fucking nose?"

The brothers stripped my clothes from me faster than any girl I'd ever slept with and left them in a pile on the floor. I tried reaching for my nose to pinch off the blood flow, but Cory grabbed my hands and wouldn't let me use them. Cody grabbed my legs, and they lifted me from the floor. They slowed when we descended the basement steps. Neither of them paused to turn on a light, so they slowed down even more since they couldn't see where they were going.

I said, "Good thing y'all can't see my pecker. Hate to

think what would happen to me if y'all could see how pretty it is. Cody, I know you'd like it especially. The way you've been looking at me all night's made it shrivel up some. Don't look as impressive as when your mama's playing with it."

That got me tossed on the floor, and a boot toe punted me right between my ribs. I balled up on the floor the way a roly-poly does when a child pokes it with a stick. Cody pinned me there, and Cory stumbled around the basement looking for the box.

Cory said, "Why's it so damn dark down here?"

"Just hurry up and find the damn thing."

"I'm trying."

"It wasn't never over there. It's over there."

"Where?"

"There."

"Where?"

"I'm pointing right at it."

"Unless you plan on pulling a flashlight from your asshole, I can't see where the fuck you're pointing, Cody."

"You ain't even close to it," a woman said, "y'all moved it over here by the baptismal tub."

"Didn't nobody tell you to speak, bitch," Cory said, "don't say another word unless you want me shutting that mouth for you?"

A short silence fell over the room, and Cody said, "Get over here and help me pick him up."

Cory marched across the basement and grabbed me by the ankles. They moved faster now that they knew where they were going. When we reached the box, they body-slammed me into the side of it. Cody let my legs go, said, "Let me get the keys."

I didn't lay there long before the lid of the box got

tossed open, and they tried to shove me down inside.

Somebody grabbed me by the nuts and squeezed until I puked some and collapsed into the freezer box. The lid slapped shut, and I heard the lock click into place. Cody got the last word in when he said, "Goddamn, now I gotta wash my fucking hands."

9.

Being crammed inside a freezer ain't a damn bit comfortable. Moving around took all my effort, but after some work, I was able to get balled up and produce some warmth that way. I laid there and tried coming up with an idea of how I'd escape, but my options weren't stepping forward from the lineup when asked. If I got a moment where I evened the numbers, it would be my best chance. I started thinking of how I could get in touch with Marshall when there was a knock on the side of the freezer.

"Can you hear me in there?" It was the woman. She was hard to hear through the freezer's stainless-steel body and however many inches of styrofoam. I figured her to be afraid of somebody hearing her make a sound.

"Barely," I said back. "The motor's too loud."

"Let me see if I can unplug it." She started grunting and cussed herself for having short arms, and then the motor cut off. "Got it."

"Maybe it won't be so cold in here now."

I was speaking more to myself than I was to her, but she said, "Might take an hour or so for it to warm up in there but hold tight."

"Thanks." I didn't know what else to say to her besides that and got quiet. It was hard carrying on a conversation when you couldn't see who you were talking to.

She asked, "They just get you, or they got Marshall too?"

Her asking personal questions made me realize the voice sounded familiar. Being inside the freezer muffled it too much for me to recognize it with any certainty. I asked, "Who am I talking to?"

"You can't tell who you're talking to?"

I couldn't tell if she got insulted by my question or just fooling with me, and I said, "I'm stuck inside a damn freezer. Nothing don't sound right."

"It's Andrea, Mack. Andrea Lewellen."

If I could've sat up inside the freezer, I would have. "What the hell they got you locked up in this basement for?"

Andrea didn't answer, and I had to ask her if she was still there. "I'm here," she said and then got quiet again. The quiet continued for a few minutes, and then she answered me. "They got me down here because of what you and your brother did."

This time it was my turn to respond in silence. I was trying to think of what reason the preacher could have for locking her in this basement. "What do you mean you're down here cause of what me and Marshall done? You're the one who caught us stealing that money and called the preacher on us."

There was a thump against the freezer. Andy said, "Brother Jessup claimed God spoke to him and revealed to him the whole thing was a setup. Said Deddy came up with the idea to have y'all steal the money and used me calling him to make it look like we tried to stop y'all."

"What the hell kinda bullshit is that?" I asked. "Y'all didn't have nothing to do with it."

"We told Brother Jessup. He didn't wanna hear it. Said the Spirit of Deception was using us to work against God's plan."

"Spirit of Deception?"

"That's the preacher's way of saying we were lying."

"Then why the hell don't he just say that?" I asked, but Andy didn't answer. She'd gone quiet on me again. I understood why. These were shitty circumstances to have to catch up under, "Where's your deddy, Andy?"

I thought I heard her cry.

"They killed him, Mack."

Harper Lewellen didn't always like me, but he was a good man. There wasn't nobody in Tugalo County who had a bad word to say about him, especially my Deddy. Harp was there for Deddy whenever Deddy was around, and hearing that old Harp got murdered made me mad enough to shit nails. "What the hell you mean they killed him?"

Andrea couldn't tell the story for crying, so she took a minute, but her voice was still shaky. "The preacher came to our house a couple of nights after y'all did. Said God spoke to him about us being in on it and that we needed to face judgment. Deddy told him to get off our property, or he was going to get his gun, but the Elis didn't let that happen. They beat Deddy up so bad his own feet couldn't carry him, and they dragged him to the truck. They brought us here to the church basement. Brother Jessup said Deddy needed to get baptized, but this wasn't no baptism you read about in the Bible. He called it the Baptism of Serpents. Said God revealed it to him in a vision. Spoke to him about how Deddy was a deceiver like the serpent was for Eve. Said Deddy needed to get baptized among his own kind and let them decide the fate he should suffer."

I let her take her time. I couldn't hardly hear her breathing. She went on, "Mack, they filled this baptismal tub with snakes. I ain't never seen anything like it. There were pinewood boxes of 'em all around this room, and they were all stirred up. I still can't get the hissing outta my head. The Elis tossed Deddy into that tub like it wasn't nothing. Didn't even give him a chance to beg. Deddy's always been fearful of snakes, and they started pouring box after box in on top of him. He tried climbing out, but they ate him up. That hiss they make as they strike didn't ease up for a second. I ain't never heard him scream like that. Something came outta him that was otherworldly. It scares me to think about it. They locked me up down here after that. Left them snakes down here for days and made me listen to 'em slither around. I'm just glad they're gone."

She let out a sigh clear enough to hear inside the freezer and finished. "I've been needing to get that off my chest. Sorry it had to be you, Mack. Don't be mad, but I'm going to sleep. I'm exhausted now."

I don't know if Andy slept, but she didn't say another word to me. I know I never caught a wink.

10.

The basement light blinded me, and I couldn't see shit. My arms worked like rolled putty, and my legs gave out when Cody dragged me from the box and tossed me at the preacher's feet. Randy Jessup handed me my jeans and said, "Put these on, friend. I don't want to have to see your indecency."

I looked down at my shriveled member and smiled with all my teeth. "You afraid of looking at my pecker because you might like what you see, preacher?"

Andy laughed. We both looked over at her, huddled up in a corner, and she covered her mouth. She'd got stripped down to her underwear - and a shackle locked around her ankle. A big chain laid on top of a bolt next to her, and she sat on top of a sleeping bag.

"Why ain't you got no clothes on?" I asked her.

Randy Jessup answered for her. "God spoke in the book of Isaiah, 'Thy nakedness shall be uncovered, yea, thy shame shall be seen.'"

"Go piss up a rope," I said before the preacher could go on. His eye ignited in a burst of anger, and he nodded his head. A big paw grabbed me by the back of my neck and squeezed until I thought the vertebrates would splinter. A heavy fist found the same spot the toe of the boot tenderized the night before, and I fell. I didn't know if anything got broken, but I could hardly breathe and wheezed in a little bit of air at a time.

Andy said, "Keep your goddamn hands off him."

The anger in Randy Jessup's eye spread across his face. Andy thrust her hands up, but he shoved them into her lap, and smacked her. Her head snapped to the side and the rest of her body went with it.

"Hey, preacher," I hollered, "remember last night when I guessed you like to prey on defenseless women? It's something sexual for you, ain't it? That the only way you can raise the steeple? Be honest now, preacher, God'll—"

Cody Eli kicked me so hard I clamped my mouth shut for fear of my soul floating out otherwise. A hand grabbed me by the hair, and Randy Jessup took center stage wearing a new eyepatch with a flaming dove from Heaven.

"I would not normally say this, but I'm going to revel in what the Lord has in store for you today. Maybe you'll quit all that foolish talk and crudeness." Randy Jessup shook my hair and scalp loose from his fingers. "Cody, make him get dressed and bring him upstairs. Cory's waiting for us."

Cody snatched me from the floor and shoved my jeans in my face. I knew he was looking for a reason to hurt me, and I didn't know if I could take another beating. I took my time slipping each leg into my jeans, but Cody didn't even give me a chance to zip.

Randy Jessup sat next to the big wooden torture device Christ got crucified to death upon. He'd crossed one leg over the other and flipped the onion skins of his Bible. He didn't seem to be looking for any particular scripture and put it away when we came into the room. Cory Eli sat in a pew at the front of the church and turned to see us come down the aisle. He stood like he was waiting to see the blushing bride-to-be, then the preacher walked down the steps from the altar.

A bench press stood in the middle of the floor with a towel draped over the end of it. Jugs of water sat on the floor next to it. Cory looked like Rambo, fresh out of ammo with a belt draped over each shoulder. Cody body-slammed me on the floor and bowled me onto the bench. Cory came in while his brother held me down and strapped a belt across my chest and thighs. They were buckled in so tight I could feel the circulation getting cut off to my hands and feet. The preacher stepped into my line of sight, and that flaming dove floated above me.

"Nazis would slit your belly and leave you in the company of a hog. Vietcong like to tap bamboo reeds under your fingernails. Hell of a way to get gangrene. Arabs will take a set of jumper cables to your privates and try to figure out which one was positive and which was negative. But there are no heathens in the house of the Lord."

Randy Jessup bent to lift one of those jugs from the floor. Cory Eli took the towel and pulled it across my face like they did to that fatass in *Full Metal Jacket*. The preacher said, "We left here last night and went looking for your brother, but he wasn't at that bar in Blackwood where Jessa picked you up at. Wasn't at your trailer when we rolled by there. Even checked your mama's place."

Hearing Randy Jessup mention my mama made me go Mister Hyde against the belts. Then either Tweedle-Dee or Tweedle-Dum flipped the foot of the bench into the air, and my brain went like your belly does when you drive your car over a hill too fast, and it makes you float from your seat. I heard the lid pop off the jug and water gush. It soaked the towel, filled my mouth, and I couldn't recruit the right brain cells to breathe through my nose. It felt like someone tried to jam a mophead down my throat. Waterboarding makes every drowning scenario you had as a kid come to fruition at the exact same moment. If the preacher planned on killing me, I wished he'd do it a little faster.

Then it all stopped.

Cory Eli pulled the towel from my face, and Cody set the bench flush on the floor.

Air rushed to its rightful place. Randy Jessup looked down at me with a sadistic smile on his face. "Where's your brother hiding, Mack?"

I shook my head back and forth and let them know I didn't know where Marshall was. The preacher's cruel smile turned belligerent. "Your lies won't help your brother none, friend. And it surely doesn't help your situation." He lifted another jug and the towel got slapped across my face again, and the bottom of the bench flew back into the air, sharper the second time, so that my mouth filled instantly and rushed down into my nose, making my nostrils burn like I was smoking a roach with an acetylene torch.

That feeling clawed through my body until I begged whoever was listening to die. But death lingered off in the distance and let me suffer hell. The bench dropped to the floor, and the towel fell away.

"Where's your brother?"

I couldn't tell him they should check Brystal's place,

there was no way I was bringing her into this. I leaned as far forward as the belt allowed and spit in his eyeball.

"Go get the girl."

11.

ory dumped the bench and undid the buckles. The belts fell to the floor, but I couldn't get away. Cory grabbed one of them, wrapped it around his big fist, and lashed it across my back. My whole body knotted while a new kernel of pain burrowed its roots into me. He grabbed me by a handful of hair and dragged me up to the altar. Cory shoved me into the chair the preacher'd been sitting in before and reached into his back pocket for a pair of handcuffs, and cuffed my wrists to the arms of the preacher's golden throne. The cuffs scraped away the latex spray paint.

Andy looked like hell. I didn't dare imagine what they'd done to her. She didn't say a word when Cody led her down the aisle of the sanctuary. When they reached the front of the church, the preacher returned wearing a polo shirt with the church's name over his heart. He'd cleaned himself up. Andy wilted like a dying flower when he walked near. He stopped before he reached the end of the aisle, took in the whole scene, rubbing his hands together and humming the tune for *The Old Rugged Cross*.

"Sister Andrea, it pains me to have to bring you

before the Lord in this manner, but our friend there has no care for your safety and refuses to cooperate with me. The Lord spoke to me and let me know the only way he'll learn is by watching you suffer. I must act as the Lord directs me."

Andy collapsed. Cody tried catching her, but he wasn't swift enough, so she dropped to the floor. She slapped the ground beneath her with everything she had, using nothing more than her right earlobe and that same cheek. The preacher walked the short distance to the front of the church and took Andy by the arm. She was slow getting back to her feet, but Randy Jessup helped her stand and put a hand on both her shoulders.

She shook all over but didn't have enough strength left over to look the preacher in the face. "What have I told you about being so dramatic, Sister Andrea? It doesn't bring you any favor from the Lord."

Andy cried into her hands. The preacher's face turned callous, and he gripped her shoulders until droplets of blood rolled off the tips of his fingernails. When Andy could speak, she said, "Please don't hurt me, Brother Jessup. I'll do whatever God commands, but I don't wanna be hurt no more."

"This ain't got nothing to do with nobody but me and you. Just let her go."

The preacher shoved Andy onto the bench so hard it nearly tipped. "Friend, Peter wrote in his second epistle that God did not spare the angels who sinned but cast them down to hell and delivered them into chains of darkness to be held for the day of judgment. I will not sin against God and suffer the same fate. No, sir. Just as Jesus said, 'He that is faithful in that which is least is faithful also in much.'"

The Elis grabbed her by the arms and legs. Her screams cut through his preaching, and she fought to get away from them. Cory grabbed Andy by a handful of hair and jerked her over. They stretched her across the bench, and Cody pinned her to it. Cory cinched the first belt so tight across her chest it flattened her tits. The preacher stood over her and ran the tips of his fingers through her hair. Andy shuddered at his touch and winced when the second belt got strapped across her thighs. Randy held me in a gaze to make certain he had my devotion. Fire licked his good eye matching the flaming dove stitched into his eye patch, then he blinked and left that eye closed while he told the Elis to get where he needed them. He flicked the lid of a water jug with a quick flick of the thumb.

● ● ●

Andy finally went limp. Cody dropped the foot of the bench, and Cory jerked the towel from her face. Randy Jessup slipped his fingers into the crook of Andy's neck to check her pulse. "Take her back to the basement," he said to the Elis, "when you're done with her, come back and get him. I need to prepare my sermon for tomorrow."

12.

The Elis hauled me down to the basement. I stopped at the bottom of the stairs to look for Andy. She'd been tossed into the basement corner and left like a crumpled pile of dirty laundry. Cody shoved me, and I tripped my way over to the freezer. Cory lifted the lid. "Get inside."

"Wait," Cody said, "take your pants off first."

I turned so he could watch me do it and said, "Your mama's gone be pissed if I get freezer burn on my pecker."

Andy didn't laugh at that. It got a rise out of Cory, though. "Say another word about my mama and see if I don't beat the shit outta you."

Cody flinched at his brother's language. "Just get in the freezer. It ain't gotta be no worse than that."

I let the corner of my mouth curl into one of those fuck-yourself-smirks meant just for Cory. "Get in the goddamn freezer."

Cody flipped me inside like a dead carcass needing hiding.

The lid slammed on my head and shut with a thud. The chain jingled around, and the lock clicked into place, and the motor snored to life. I waited for what seemed an appropriate amount of time to call for Andy. I said her name big and loud and made sure she could hear me over the motor, but she offered no reply.

Andy could hold a grudge better than any girl I knew, but this wasn't like her - even when I made her so mad she'd tell me she didn't want to see me again, we'd keep talking, it might be a few days before one of us made contact with the other, but there'd be a phone call, or we'd just so happen to be at the same place at the same time, I wanted her to know that I wasn't lying when I told the preacher I didn't know where Marshall was, the last thing I wanted was for any harm to come to her, but she wouldn't answer me and I hollered her name until my throat was raw.

If the preacher was going to keep his word, I'd be dead by tomorrow afternoon. I needed her to know I was sorry.

"Andy," I hollered her name so loud I could hear myself scream into both of my ears, "if you ain't gone answer me I need you to listen to me. If I could've known the shit storm taking that money would cause I'd've never let Marshall talk me into it. We didn't even mean to take enough for y'all to notice. I wish to God, you'd've never found us in that goddamn hole. If I'm able to get my hands on that preacher, I'm gone do it, by God. I need to know you're alright, Andy. Please knock on the side of the freezer or tell me to shut up or you hate me. That's all I need."

If Andy heard a word I said, she never let me know it. She left me there in the clanging silence of the freezer, and I couldn't blame her. None of what happened was any of her fault, and she was better off leaving me to freeze. The cold made some poor company, but I did my best to get comfortable with it. I maneuvered around until I got back into the fetal position like the night before and did my best to generate some warmth. There would be nobody to unplug the freezer for me tonight, and I was worried about hypothermia or frostbite. It'd make a shitty end to my story if I ended up freezing to death.

Freezers are a lot like casinos with no clocks or windows - I lost all sense of time. I thought it must be morning when I heard some banging around the basement. I thought the Elis must be coming for me when Andy hollered. It was the first time I heard her voice since the afternoon before. I yelled Andrea's full name, but she wasn't paying attention to me. She begged whoever came down to the basement to take her out of here, and I couldn't figure out what was going on.

The lock jangled, and the lid slung open.

"Goddamn, Coy," my brother said.

13.

Marshall pulled me out of the freezer by my arms, and I ran to Andy, but he wouldn't let me. My jeans got shoved into my hands, but Marshall ushered me to the basement steps, where a big fucker waited for us. Seeing Caudell Clark standing there reminded me of all the bar fights he got into for fun, using mangled bodies to mop up bloodstained floors. He made the Elis look small. It made me nervous as to what my brother had gotten us into.

I stopped to put on my jeans but ignored Marshall when he said to keep moving. He didn't want to hear what I had to say, but I made him listen. Words grated on my throat when I spoke. It sounded like Beelzebub did the talking for me. "We gotta get Andy outta here."

"That ain't happening, Coy," Marshall said, "now let's get outta here."

"Marshall," I said, "that preacher's been putting her through all kinds of hell. God knows what he'll do when he finds y'all took me."

Caudell answered me this time. He didn't leave room for argument. He put a catcher's mitt of a hand on my shoulder, and his Black knuckles looked busted from pounding faces. "The girl ain't coming. You're all I was told to come here and get."

"Told to come here and get me?" I said, then turned to my brother. "What did you do, Marshall?"

Marshall shoved me past Caudell and up the steps. "Bitch at me later, Coy, we need to get the fuck outta here."

I stumbled up the first few steps and caught my balance on the handrail. "Keep your goddamn hands off me, Marshall. Answer my questions or I ain't going nowhere."

Caudell's voice outweighed my brother's. "Tell you everything you need to know back at the truck. Now go."

The basement door got busted into kindling. It made me sick leaving Andy.

We went through the side door of the sanctuary and headed up the aisle between the pews. That oversized wooden cross loomed over us like an omen of doom. The front doors were missing from the hinges, and glass trailed all the way out to the parking lot. I didn't walk no further. Marshall said, "C'mon, Coy, what the hell!"

"I ain't got shoes on, Marshall. Want my feet cut all to hell?"

Marshall looked at the ground and turned his back to me, leaned forward a little.

"Goddamn, Marshall, I ain't jumping on your back."

"Then bleed, Coy." Marshall threw his hands in the air and tried to keep his voice low.

Caudell's boots munched glass. "Y'all get this figured out. We ain't waiting on y'all forever."

"Who's we?" I said, but Caudell climbed into the passenger's side of the Bronco and slammed the door.

I raised my eyebrows at Marshall and threw my hands to the side.

"Let's get in the truck, and I'll explain everything to you."

"Why the hell're you so anxious to get when there's a defenseless woman chained up in that basement?"

"Goddamn, Coy, you miss that freezer?"

Marshall ran a hand over his scruff. "That defenseless woman is the reason for this whole shit storm. Don't you remember her calling the preacher? She can rot in that goddamn basement."

"Marshall," I said, but the Bronco's horn let us know it was time to go.

"C'mon, Coy," Marshall said, "they'll leave us if we carry on."

He turned his back to me, leaned forward for me again, and I hopped on. My brother carried me to the passenger's side of the truck, and I slid across the backseat behind the driver, and Marshall got in beside me.

Roy Bohannon turned in the driver's seat and looked at me with one of his country-mile grins. "What you know good, Mack?"

"What the fuck you done got us into, Marshall?"

PART THREE

Mine eyes have seen the glory
Of the coming of the Lord;
He is trampling out the vintage
Where the grapes of wrath are stored;
He hath loosed the fateful lightning
Of His terrible swift sword;
His truth is marching on.

1.

Everybody called Roy Bohannon Peanut. He drove with one arm slung out the driver's side window and the other propped atop of the steering wheel. As soon as we left the church, he put on a Hank Williams Jr. CD and blasted it through the speakers so loud nobody could talk, and Peanut sang along with Bocephus - sang extra loud with every chorus and glanced in the mirror to see if any of us sang too.

He drove us out to the Bohannon compound where the empire had got run since his great granddeddy was alive. It stood deep out in the woods of Tugalo County, where Albermarle Mountain overshadowed the property, its radio towers a pair of blinking stars. Nobody went out there unless Peanut knew beforehand. Otherwise, people who came out uninvited got fed to Caudell and disappeared in the mountains. When Peanut turned onto the dirt road, he turned the stereo down and pulled over.

He turned and pushed his ball cap back on his head, looked at me and my brother but spoke to me specifically. "Katie's got y'all a room made up, but y'all're gone have to share. She wanted y'all's mama to have a room to herself and not have to worry 'bout being decent 'round y'all. Deddy is living with me now, and he ain't none too happy 'bout y'all staying here. If he runs his mouth, ignore him."

When Peanut finished talking, he slapped Caudell on the shoulder and smiled. "This's gone be like old times again, y'all. I can't wait."

He turned the volume knob on the stereo all the way to the right and jacked the music up. Hank Jr's Alabama drawl echoed through the backcountry, and the Bronco bounced through every rut in the road, shaking me around the backseat, and Marshall kept an iron grip on the door handle. Caudell leaned back in his seat and never once got jostled by Peanut's driving. The Bronco slowed to another stop, and we approached a chain-link fence. A couple of boys sat in a pickup truck parked alongside the road, and they got out when they saw us. They brought automatic rifles and walked over to the driver's side. Peanut turned the music down and said, "What you know good, boys?"

One of them leaned into Peanut's window. "Been a quiet night, boss. Fixing to fall asleep."

Peanut leaned away from the kid and put a hand over his nose. "Goddamn, Wiley, when's the last time you brushed your teeth? Smells like you let Tommy over there take a shit in your mouth."

Tommy slapped the top of the Bronco and laughed at the insult, and Wiley wilted. He took a step away from the truck, and Tommy took his spot. Tommy said, "He doesn't even like it when I wipe, boss. Likes to lick up them dingleberries and everything."

Peanut pushed Tommy out of his widow. "Don't be so goddamn crude, Tommy. You always take shit too far."

Peanut hitched a thumb in my direction. "Got a new face y'all need to remember. Y'all see him around, do me a favor, and don't fucking shoot him. Understand?"

The boys nodded that they did, and Peanut motioned for one of them to open the gate. Tommy ran over to it, and Peanut said, "I'll send Katie down with some Colgate, Wiley. Help that breath some."

Wiley nodded. "I'd appreciate that, boss." Then, "And, hey, Peanut?"

"Yeah, boy?"

"I ain't never really actually let Tommy take a shit in my mouth."

"Hell, I know that," Peanut shifted the Bronco into drive, "I'm fucking with you. But, Wiley, one thing I ain't fucking with you about is sleeping on the job. If I ever catch you, you'll answer to Caudell."

Peanut gunned the Bronco before Wiley could answer and waved at Tommy as we drove by. I turned to watch the boys roll the gate shut as soon as we were through. Neither of them could be older than sophomores and had no idea what kind of man they were dealing with. When I turned back, Peanut smiled in the rearview mirror, and I looked beyond him. The Bohannon home sat upon the highest point on the property and gave a pretty view of the Blue Ridge Mountains. Floodlights lit the driveway up like a night game, and Peanut parked next to an Excursion. Peanut cut the engine, kicked the door open, and slid out in one smooth motion.

"Y'all come have a beer."

We followed him around to the front porch, and Buford was sitting there waiting for us. The old bastard looked at me, mirroring my disgust. It should've been him locked up in Sweetwater instead of my Deddy. He looked away before I did, and Peanut sat next to him. "What you know good, Deddy?"

Buford curled up a lip and spat out into the yard. "We're almost outta beer. I probably oughta go get some."

2.

Y'all have a seat."

Marshall did like he was told and took the rocking chair next to Peanut's. He slung a leg over the arm of the chair like he belonged and looked at me funny. I kept standing, leaned back against the porch banister, and propped my elbows on it.

Marshall said, "Hey, Coy, don't be so damn rude. Take a seat like Peanut asked."

I ignored my brother and kept my eyes focused on the big man sitting across from me. The hard features of his face got hidden in the shadows of his baseball cap, but his smile flickered like a razor blade in the light. What actually went on in his mind was hidden by that full-toothed grin, but Peanut waved my brother off.

"Hell, Marshall," Peanut said, "if Mack was cooped up in a freezer like Cody Eli said, he's probably happy to stretch his legs. Let him stand if he wants to."

"Why'd the Elis let y'all know where I was?" I asked.

The question made an Elvis Presley smirk curl Marshall's upper lip, and Peanut pushed his hat back on the crown of his head. He said, "Caudell has a way of getting information outta people."

"Peanut?"

He shrugged.

I crossed my arms over my chest and flinched. All the beatings I'd taken over the past couple of days were catching up to me. It hurt no matter how I stood, and moving around only made it worse. Marshall asked, "You all right, Coy?"

Peanut said, "Looks like hell, don't he?"

I said, "I just need some sleep."

Peanut said, "I'll holler for Katie if you want. Have her take you up to your bedroom. Get you set up for the night."

"That's all right," I said. "I need to know what you plan to do about the preacher."

Peanut rocked back in his chair, and an unsteady silence fell over the three of us. He put his hands behind his head, locked his fingers together, and used his hands as a headrest. He took in a deep breath, and his belly expanded like a balloon. After he breathed out, he said, "Listen, Mack, the preacher's on my priority list, but he ain't nowhere near the top. He's got friends who complicate things."

"Who?"

The question made Peanut uneasy. Marshall must not have known either because he turned in his chair and watched Peanut rock. He got out of his chair and walked to the end of the porch. He took a can of long-cut out of his back pocket and popped the lip a couple of times. Peanut took a large pinch from the can, packed his bottom lip, and spat.

"Kendall Murdoch."

The name didn't register with me.

"Who's that?" Marshall asked.

"Y'all know who he is," Peanut said, "probably seen his damn campaign signs all over the county. He's running for senate."

"I've seen him on TV," Marshall said, "like a damn used car salesman."

"You ain't far off," Peanut said.

"What's his connection with Randy Jessup?" I asked.

Peanut sat back down and rocked back to spit in the trash can.

I waited Peanut out, and he smiled. He said, "That preacher's using his church to launder money for him."

"Goddamn," Marshall said, "I knew that fucking preacher was crooked."

"That's where Harper Lewellen got all the money," I said.

"Sure is," Peanut said, "and y'all're gone help me get it."

Marshall looked over at me and waited to see how I'd react. His forehead wrinkled, and I understood the deal he'd made with Peanut to get me out of the church.

"I need something for me first," I said.

Peanut's eyes narrowed, and he spat in the trash can.

I finally took a seat in Buford's rocking chair. The seat was still warm from when he'd been sitting in it, and I propped my elbows on the arms and ran my hands through my hair. "Andy Lewellen."

"Goddamn," Marshall said.

Peanut looked over at my brother and then back at me. "Explain."

"After we stole that money, the preacher killed her deddy and chained her up in that basement. Now that I ain't there no more and the Elis ain't around, she's probably gone suffer the same fate as Harp."

Peanut leaned over to me. "Explain to me how that's my problem?"

"It's not. It's mine."

Peanut leaned back in his chair, and Marshall said, "I don't see how it's your goddamn problem, Coy."

Peanut asked Marshall, "She's the one that called the preacher on y'all?"

Marshall said, "Gave us up like prom pussy."

"So let her stink the place up," Peanut said.

Marshall said, "That's what I told him."

"I can't do that."

Buford and Caudell were on the way back with a cooler full of beer, and the discussion was over.

"Where's mama?" I asked.

"She's done asleep," Marshall said. "I had to medicate her when she found out where you was. She got Deddy's rifle and was fixing to shoot the preacher, God, and everybody unless they let you go. You'll see her in the morning."

"I'm gone go ahead and get some sleep then. I'm 'bout dead on my feet."

"You ain't even gone have one beer with me?" Peanut asked.

"Not tonight."

"Tomorrow then."

3.

The smell of bacon frying teased me from my dreams. Sunshine lit the room just enough for me to see Marshall wasn't in his bed. I didn't know if he'd ever come to it. As soon as my head hit the pillow, I died to the world. I kicked the blankets to the foot of the bed and rolled out of it. My pants hung over a bedpost, and I put them on. I needed to find a shirt to wear, but all I found were kids' clothes in the drawers I checked. Hopefully, Katie didn't mind me walking around half-naked until I got some other clothes.

I followed the smell of bacon. The whole house was quiet except for the grease popping, and Peanut turned when I walked in the room. He wore the same clothes from the night before and still had his baseball cap on. His country mile grin stretched across his face.

"What you know good, Mack?"

"Morning, Peanut," I said.

"Thought you might be hungry. I cooked us up some bacon and eggs and got some biscuits in the oven. Hope you don't mind they ain't homemade. Katie's the one who gets into all that."

"Smells good."

I took a seat at the kitchen table and watched Peanut flip bacon. He did it quickly - and then walked over to the refrigerator. He opened the door, grabbed two beers, and brought me one over. He sat it down in front of me, and I looked at it and then up at him. His ball cap didn't hide his features like it did the night before. It looked like there was some excitement there, like a little kid running out to recess.

"I told you last night you'd drink a beer with me."

"What time is it?"

"Beer o'clock."

"Katie don't mind?"

"Katie's dropping the kids off at school and won't never know 'bout one beer." Peanut returned to the bacon and removed the skillet from the eye. He set it off to the side to let the cast iron cool and forked the bacon from it. Once he finished, he opened the oven to check on the biscuits. "They're almost done."

"Where is everybody?"

"That beer's getting warm." Peanut held his can but hadn't drunk yet. I realized he was waiting on me and popped mine open. He took a big step across the kitchen, touched the rim of his can to mine, said, "Cheers."

We drank long and hard, but Peanut chugged his and checked the biscuits one last time. He grabbed a dish-towel to take them from the stove, and we both made a plate. Peanut took a seat across from me at the table and started talking with his mouth full.

"I sent Caudell and your brother into town with your mama. They're grabbing you some clothes and whatever else you'll need to stay here for a while. Randy Jessup's out searching for y'all. This's the safest place for you." Peanut swallowed what he'd chewed and shoveled more food into his mouth. He kept talking, "I made Deddy take the kids to school with Katie. She's taking him to pick up his medicine and run errands. This way, we can talk."

I took a swig of my beer, chased it with some bacon, stabbed the eggs with my fork. Peanut watched me eat and waited for me to swallow. He wouldn't look away from me until I asked, "What do you wanna talk about, Peanut?"

"Mack, c'mon, we known each other since we was little kids."

I stabbed the eggs so hard my fork clanked against the plate. "That goddamn money."

Peanut sat back in his chair and looked at me the way a dog does when it can't understand its master's tone.

"All you and my brother are worried about is some fucking money, and there's a girl out there that's probably gone die." I dropped my fork onto the plate and pushed it away from me.

Peanut reached over for my last piece of bacon. "It ain't the money, Mack, it's the damage it'll do to Kendall Murdoch. I jerk that rug from underneath him, and he won't be able to stand up to me."

"Why do you need me and my brother, Peanut?" I asked. "You got a whole army of men that can help you get that money. Hell, Caudell could do it all by himself."

Peanut all but licked his plate clean and fingered the few crumbs. He licked them from the tip of his finger and said, "It ain't that I need y'all's help, Mack. It's that y'all're indebted to me, and this's how you'll work it off. If y'all feel like this's something you wanna do more of, we can work an arrangement out. I feel like I owe y'all that."

"What do you mean, owe us this?"

"You know things didn't end well between your deddy and mine. This's always been just as much y'all's business as it is mine. I wanna make things right between us if you'll let me, Mack. Bring the Dooleys back into the fold."

I leaned across the table. Peanut smelled like bacon grease and cheap beer. I could tell he didn't like me being so close. "I don't want shit to do with this business. I made my mind up about that when my Deddy got locked up in Sweetwater."

A car door slammed. I got up from the table, but Peanut grabbed my wrist. Before I could take it back, he said, "It's fine if you don't wanna work with me, Mack, but you still got this debt to work off."

4.

I stood under the showerhead and let hot water wash away the last few days.

Dirt swirled around the shower drain, and I scrubbed my skin until it was raw. I stood under a cold shower until all of me trembled.

I dressed in the clothes Mama bought for me and left my towel in a basket. Katie was around the house somewhere, and I did my best to stay out of her way. The radio played in one of the kids' bedrooms, and she sang along.

Buford squatted outside Mama's door when I walked up. He acted like he didn't see me and sneered at me when Mama said 'hey.' "There something I can help you with, boy?"

I stepped into the old man's space and said, "You can start by getting outta my way."

Mama spoke up with a voice warm as honey. "Give us just a few minutes here, Buford, and come back by. You can finish telling me that story about Walt. I ain't never heard it before."

Buford gave Mama a nod and started to leave when I said, "You need to keep my Deddy's name outta your mouth."

Buford swung around in the hallway and put a finger in my chest. "It's a shame your deddy ain't here to take care of your mama. She's a pretty one."

I grabbed Buford by the wrist. He jerked, but I tightened my grip until weakness streaked across his face. All it would've took was for me to give it a twist, and Buford would've went to the emergency room. But Mama stopped me.

"Mackenzie Walter Dooley, what's done go into you, son? Let him go right now."

I didn't do what Mama told me, but I loosened my grip enough for Buford to retrieve his hand. He massaged his wrist as I stepped inside Mama's bedroom and slammed the door.

Mama slapped me when I turned toward her. Tears made my vision bleary, and my cheek burned. She said, "What the hell's done got into, son? You don't come into somebody's house acting that way. Not after what they done for you."

"What they done for us?" I swiped the back of an arm across my eyes. "It ain't like Peanut was acting out of the goodness of his heart, Mama. He told me we was gone have to work it off as a debt."

"I don't like it no more than you do, Mack," Mama left me by the door and sat on the edge of her bed, "but it's the situation you and Marshall got yourselves into."

"So you want us to go off and do Peanut's bidding then?"

"It's better than y'all being left at the mercy of that preacher."

"You don't know what kinda trouble Peanut's gone ask us to cause."

"But it's trouble I know, son. Ever since the day your

deddy got tangled up with Buford." Mama shook her head like it might change the past. "At least if y'all are working with Peanut, I know y'all got his protection. Y'all ain't got that on your own. And it scares me to think of what that preacher might be capable of."

I sat down next to Mama and kept my eyes on the floor. The words I wanted to say got stuck inside me, and I had to pry them out. "He killed Harper Lewellen, Mama."

Mama gasped, and I looked over at her. A hand covered her mouth, and she looked at me like I jumped out from around a corner and spooked her. She tried speaking, but the words came out in a sputter.

I went on without waiting for her to get it together. "Andy Lewellen told me. The preacher's keeping her captive in the church basement, and I think he'll kill her next. He'll want to after what Marshall did to get me free. I gotta get her, Mama."

Mama's hand dropped into her lap, and her eyes got stern. "How you gone do it, Mackenzie?"

"I've tried asking Peanut to help me, but he won't do it. He's more worried about getting the preacher's money than helping Andy." My eyes turned back to the floor. "I'll have to do it on my own."

"Son—"

"I can't let him kill her, Mama," I gripped a handful of covers until it made my knuckles swell, "it's my fault she's down there. I shouldn't've never let Marshall talk me into stealing that money. I gotta go get her out."

Mama sighed.

"Don't try and talk me out of it."

Mama took my chin and made me look at her. "You hush and let me talk now. Your Uncle Arlo got himself into a situation one time where your deddy did everything he could to get him out of it. You know how I feel about Arlo Burke, and I told your deddy not to do none of what he was thinking. He would've listened to me, too, but it would've eat him up on the inside. Arlo is his best friend, and your deddy couldn't not help him. I ended up telling your deddy to do what needed doing but not to get himself hurt. Told him if he did, I'd make sure it was me who put him out of his misery."

"What're you saying, Mama?"

"You know what I'm saying, Mackenzie."

5.

Marshall shook me awake late that afternoon. Outside there was an orange tint to the sky, and it looked like Albermarle Mountain was on fire. Falling asleep wasn't part of the plan. I needed a car, and figuring that out is what put me to sleep.

"Hey, Coy, why don't you come down and have a beer with us? Peanut's got some steaks on the grill and everything."

I pushed myself out of bed and stretched my back. "I think I'm good to stay here and nap. Don't really feel like being 'round nobody."

"C'mon, Coy, one beer. Come down and say hey to everybody and then you can come back up here and go back to sleep."

"Nah, I'm good. I just ain't got it in me to be 'round nobody right now."

Marshall stood and cussed. "What the hell, Coy? I ain't asking you to come down and make yourself the center of attention. Just say hey and have a beer. Let people know you're alive."

Marshall clenched his jaw and jut his chin out. He turned for the door, and I thought he was leaving, but he closed it.

"You're making this real goddamn hard on me, Mack."

My brother never called me by anything but the nickname Deddy gave me when I was little. It was such a seldom occurrence for my given name to come out of Marshall's mouth that I sometimes wondered if he even knew it. Hearing it now made me all kinds of curious.

"What the hell's so hard about all this, Marshall?"

"Coy, we got a chance here to get back in good with some people that could help us for a long time. We could be right up there with the Bohannons in making decisions about Tugalo County."

I sat back down on my bed and said, "Marshall, you've eaten every ounce of bullshit Peanut's fed you."

"Goddammit, Coy." Marshall's voice carried throughout the bedroom. He faced the bedroom door, worried somebody might be on the other side.

"No, Marshall, you ain't thinking. Peanut's not handing you some ladder that'll get you to the top of the Kudzu Kings. He's using you. Just like his deddy did ours."

Marshall shook his head at me like this was the last letdown in a lifetime of letdowns. "I know what I'm getting myself into here and the kinda risk I'm taking. Deddy knew it too. He ain't in prison right now because Buford double-crossed him. He's sitting in that cell right now because that's what they asked of him—"

"You're right, Marshall. If there's one thing you and Deddy've always done for this family, it's let us down."

"Peanut says we're snatching the money tonight. He's got some boys the preacher called about helping him move it. If you ain't coming down to eat with us - then you need to be downstairs when it gets dark. Peanut said to make sure of it."

Marshall waited to see if I'd argue with that, and when I didn't, he backed the rest of the way out of the room and shut the bedroom door behind him.

6.

The moon shimmered outside the bedroom window. I'd been sitting in the same spot since Marshall left, but a plan finally started formulating. I knew Peanut would have somebody knocking on the bedroom door if I didn't head downstairs in the next few minutes, so I opened the bedroom door. Wiley stood in the hallway, ready to knock. My appearance startled him, and he jerked away. He tripped over his overgrown feet and caught himself against the wall.

"You alright there, Wiley?" I said. "Didn't mean to scare you like that. Just about to head down to meet with Peanut and them."

"No, sir, you're all right." Wiley took his cap off and used the back of his arm to wipe sweat from his brow. "Didn't expect you to jerk the door open when you did. Peanut says I need to not be so jumpy."

I still couldn't believe he worked security for the Bohannons. "Where's everybody meeting?"

"They're out here on the back porch. Peanut told me to grab a handful of cold beers on my way out."

"Sounds good." I let Wiley lead the way. "I'll give you a hand with them beers."

"Thank you, sir." Wiley led me past the room where Mama stayed. She'd shut the bedroom door, but I could hear the TV's canned laughter. That meant she was watching old reruns of a sitcom from the Eighties she liked.

I stopped Wiley at the stairs and put my hand out to him. He took it right away, and I gave it my hardest squeeze. His face barely flinched, and I knew he was trying to tough it out. "You ain't gotta call me sir, Wiley. My name's Mack."

"Yessir, Mr. Mack."

"Well, that's a start." I smiled, and he started to take his hand away, but I tightened my grip further, and he let out a groan. I twisted his wrist, and his voice went up in pitch, and I brought him to his knees. I wrenched his arm behind him, knocked him onto his belly, and pulled his shirt up, "What do we have here?"

Wiley couldn't answer me for the pain he was in, but I reached for the gun at the small of his back and took it out of his pants. I let go of his arm, and he rolled over on his ass and jumped to his feet. He tried for the pistol, but I shoved him into the wall. He didn't hit hard enough for it to make a bunch of noise, but he threw his hands over his head when I aimed it at him. "Boy, you need to calm your ass down right now 'fore I shoot you."

"That's my gun, Mr. Mack. Peanut'll kill us both if he finds out you took it."

I dropped the clip to make sure the thing was loaded and made sure a round got seated, keeping my aim on Wiley just to scare him. "Two things," I said. "One, this's my gun now." The kid's whole countenance shriveled. "Two, Peanut better not find out I got this gun, or it's gone be me that kills you, understand?"

Wiley's hands weren't above his head anymore. They got balled into fists when they came down in front of him. It took me a second before I believed what my eyes were seeing. "Are you fucking kidding me right now?"

"I'll fight you."

"What do you mean you'll goddamn fight me? I got a gun to your motherfucking face, son."

Wiley dropped his fists. "They'll hear it if you shoot me."

"Peanut'll come up here and shake my hand for getting rid of somebody so goddamn dumb."

"Let's go get that beer."

7.

eanut sat kicked back in his rocking chair when Wiley led me out onto the porch. The kid did a good job of acting like everything was normal and passed around everyone's beer. Marshall took one from me but walked to the other side of the porch and stood next to Caudell. Peanut noticed this, but Wiley finally made it to him with his beer. He took the can from Wiley with a swipe, popped it open, and sucked the suds from the lid.

"Goddamn, Wiley, I thought you were fixing to let me dehydrate," Peanut said.

Wiley shrugged it off and said, "Sorry, Peanut, I got yelled at by Miss Katie for walking in on the boys. Woke Ramsey up after she just got him to sleep."

"What the hell were you doing walking in on them in their playroom, Wiley? I told you upstairs." Peanut pointed above his head, and his voice raised in volume. "The upstairs bedroom. That's where I told you Mack was."

"Sorry, Peanut," the kid kept playing dumb, "I just forgot where you told me to go."

"You know what's gone happen now?" Peanut leaned

forward in his chair and was almost in Wiley's face. The kid froze the way a deer does after being spotlighted but didn't look Peanut in the eye. He looked down at his boots and did his best not to shrivel up. "You're on Buford detail until further notice. Take him to run his errands, pick up his medicine, or to hang out at the Elks Lodge. It don't make a shit to me what he tells you to do, just keep him outta my hair. And I swear to God, Wiley, if I get an earful about this from Katie, I'm gone have your ass. Hear me, boy?"

Peanut snatched Wiley by the face when he didn't answer. My whole self went stiff. I grabbed the porch banister to stay put. Caudell noticed it and kept his eyes on me. Peanut said to Wiley, "I asked you a question, boy. You answer me whenever I do that."

"Yessir." The word shot from Wiley's mouth like a dart, and he couldn't hold back the tears any longer.

Peanut held onto his face until he'd smushed it up and then shoved the kid away. The banister kept him from tumbling into the yard, and he braced himself in case there'd be a second round.

Peanut rocked back in his chair, took a long swig from his beer to settle his nerves. "Get your ass down to the gate and send Tommy up here. Let him know he'll be going with us tonight because you're too goddamn stupid to follow simple directions."

Peanut nursed his beer while he watched Wiley run down the dirt drive to the gate. He waited on Tommy before he said another word. When Tommy wandered into earshot, Peanut hollered for him to hurry his ass up. Tommy ran the rest of the way and came huffing up the porch steps.

Peanut said, "Wiley tell you why you're going with us

tonight instead of him?"

"He did."

"All right then," Peanut stood from his chair and took Tommy by the nape of the neck. "Follow the simple directions I give you, or it'll be your ass if you don't, hear me?"

"Yessir."

Peanut directed Tommy to come stand next to me and turned so we could all see him. He took a short pull of his beer and set the can on the porch rail. "Tonight'll be easy enough. The preacher's got a couple of boys working for him that're on my payroll. They been keeping an eye peeled for me and said he wants to move the cash tonight. They'll be working with a couple of boys from that church and are gone transfer the money to the old train station. We'll be there to make sure it don't make it no further than that. We'll ride in separate vehicles. I don't want us being no easy target. Mack, I already told Marshall y'all two will ride with me, and Caudell will ride with Tommy."

"I'll ride with Tommy," I said.

"Do what?" Peanut said, damn near knocking over his beer.

"Me and my brother ain't seeing eye to eye right now, and I'd rather not have to be in such close proximity to him."

Peanut sneaked around the patio furniture and eased his way over to me and looked down on me with a leery glare. "This gone cause me drama tonight, Mack?"

"It ain't."

Peanut nodded, but I could tell he wasn't totally convinced. "I ain't got no problem with you riding with Tommy, but I'll need y'all to hug it out or some shit 'fore we go anywhere."

I grabbed Marshall in my arms before he could stop me. He went stiff all over, but his pecker and I said, "Sorry, little brother," just loud enough for him to hear.

8.

Tommy followed Peanut's Bronco. He kept messing with the radio until I reached over and turned it off. He gave me a sour stare until I told him to keep his eyes on the road, which he did while he tightened his grip on the steering wheel. Peanut took us by the backroads. It's how he went anywhere. His deddy taught him to never rely on Tugalo County's main roads. The law always stuck to those. It was some Bohannon paranoia, but Peanut carried it with him and would pass it onto his sons.

The old train station wasn't too far of a drive from the church, but I wanted to make sure I could lose the Bronco when the time came.

My concentration broke when Tommy wouldn't shut up. He drummed a herky-jerky rhythm on the steering wheel and said, "I know this ain't for nothing too serious, but I figure if I do good Peanut'll take me on more jobs. Working that gate all hours of the night was 'bout to drive me crazy. I can't never sleep normal 'cause of it—"

"Hey, Tommy," I interrupted him, and he took his eyes off the road, "you wanna drive like you got some damn sense and not keep speeding up on Peanut's rear end? You're gone put your bumper through the back end of his truck if you keep driving like this."

Tommy did what I told him to, but he gave me some lip to go along with it. "You know you ain't gotta be so goddamn demanding. We're 'bout on the same level me and you, and I don't think I gotta take too many orders from you."

"Slow down some more."

"Slow down some more?"

"I wanna make sure we're following at a safe distance."

"Hell, we get anymore safe than this, and we'll lose 'em."

"Yep."

"What?"

I drew the pistol on Tommy. He did a double-take before it registered to him. He fumbled with his words, and then he said, "Ah shit."

I stuck the gun barrel in his ribs. "Just slow down little by little and then pull over to the side of the road."

We skidded along the shoulder of the road, and I cocked the hammer. "Pull over."

Tommy pulled the car onto the side of the road and, in one quick motion, shifted it into park and reached down into the side pocket of his door. I swiped the back of his head with the barrel, and he collapsed forward, knocked his head into the door, and dropped whatever he was reaching for. "Fuck." He grabbed the back of his head with both hands.

I smacked him a second time for even thinking it was a good idea attempting to draw a gun on me. It smashed his fingers, and he hollered in pain.

I reached past him, opened his door, and shoved him

out. He couldn't go nowhere because he was twisted up in his seatbelt and couldn't muster the smarts to unbuckle it. Fear is a funny thing. I put the gun barrel back in his side and did it for him.

"Is that Wiley's gun?"

I shoved the barrel hard into Tommy's ribs. "Who the fuck're you talking to?"

He answered with silence.

I jerked the door shut behind him and slid behind the steering wheel.

Tommy stood on the side of the road, a piss stain running down the front of his jeans.

9.

I gunned for the front doors through the empty church parking lot. Plywood covered the entrance, and I parked with the headlights shining into the church windows and lit the foyer. I let the gun lead me out of the car, and when I reached the plywood doorway, I checked the road.

I put a shoulder blow into the middle of a sheet of plywood and damn near ate the floor tiles inside the foyer. I caught myself on the wall and used it to get my balance, then aimed the pistol all around the room. Nobody jumped out of any dark corners or came to check out all the noise. I made my way into the church sanctuary, and that wooden cross still loomed like an unforgiving talismen and ushered me even faster toward the side door. It swung wide, and I stepped into the hallway with the pistol aimed.

The stairway reeked. It smelled the way our freezer did the one summer when our trailer lost power, and all the venison me and Marshall kept frozen from hunting season went rotten. It made my stomach curd the way milk does when it's gone sour. I pulled my shirt over my nose and mouth to keep from gagging. I slowed down some and hung the gun to my side. When I reached the bottom, my legs almost gave out on me.

The baptismal tub sat in the center of the room, and Andy's body was sunken into it. She sat up straight with her head bobbed on her shoulder - and her arms splayed over the sides. Snakes had gotten piled on top of her and molested her now and filled my ears with their hissing. Rattlers buzzed inside my head and put me into the kind of hypnotic state an addict goes into when the high rushes through their veins. Andy's skin felt cold, and my knees failed me. My tears streamed down her dirty fingers and cleaned them the way Mary Magdalene used hers to clean the feet of Jesus.

The preacher's voice interrupted my sobbing. He sang from the top of the steps, "Hang your head, Mack Dooley. Hang your head and cry." His heels stomped out a woeful rhythm as he descended the steps and rolled around the basement walls sounding like a hammer does when it strikes a nailhead. Randy Jessup's voice raised in volume, and he sang, "Hang your head, Mack Dooley. Poor boy, you're bound to die."

I turned when the preacher reached the bottom of the steps and saw him carrying a copperhead in his arms. It looked just like the one he'd killed a few nights before. Its head was aimed at me, and there was nothing but a deep void in its eyes. Randy Jessup sang a few more notes of the old Appalachian traditional and said, "It's nice of you to join me for Sister Andrea's mourning, friend. Jesus gives us comfort in the book of Matthew where He said, *'Blessed are they that mourn: for they shall be comforted.'* It's an unfortunate thing having to send her to her Heavenly Father in this manner, but you understand I could not remain in the company of a woman whose heart is snares and nets. It's as Ecclesiastes says, *'whoso pleaseth God shall escape from her; but the sinner shall be taken by her.'* It's why she lays in that tub before you. She's better off in the hands of God Almighty than remaining in her sinful ways. You, on the other hand, will not be seeing Him this day. You'll find yourself swimming in the lake of fire here shortly, friend."

Randy Jessup slung the snake at me before I could grab the gun. The copperhead hit me in the chest, and I fell back into the baptismal tub. Snakes tumbled onto the floor. I rolled out of the way, but the copperhead followed. Its mouth opened into a great maw and struck at me. Randy Jessup collected snakes from the floor and tossed them at me.

I rolled to the other side of the tub, and Randy Jessup lost sight of me and stopped throwing snakes. I pinned the copperhead to the floor by the back of the head and smashed it with an ugly crunch. I didn't let up until the snake stopped moving and Randy Jessup had a pistol trained on me.

Snakes twisted around his shoes. He stepped closer to me, kicking snakes as he went. "Here these words from the book of Ezekiel, friend. *'Now is the end come upon thee, and I will send mine anger upon thee according to thy ways, and will recompense upon thee all thine abominations.'"*

Randy Jessup put the gun against the back of my head, and I ignored him as one of his snakes slithered into my hand. I twisted around, and a bullet ricocheted off the floor, and I stabbed the snake into the meat of his thigh headfirst. The preacher hollered like the Holy Ghost possessed him and dropped the gun. Randy pummeled me with wild blows. I jacked my elbow into his chin so hard angels appeared to him.

He scrambled across the floor, laughing all the way. "Your ignorance of scripture is clear, friend. In the Gospel of Mark, Jesus spoke to His disciples and said, *'And these signs shall follow them that believe; In my name shall they cast out devils; they shall speak with new tongues; they shall take up serpents; and if they drink any deadly thing, it shall not hurt them.'* This venom shall do me no harm. My life is sustained by faith."

I let the preacher straddle me, and when he rolled me over, I aimed the pistol between his eyes and asked, "Hey, preacher, what's Jesus say about bullets?"

The back of his head crumbled, and blood rained on the floor.

10.

A few days later, when I came home from the grocery store, Peanut's Bronco was parked in my
driveway. I pulled in next to him, and he wasn't
sitting in the driver's seat. I grabbed my groceries from
the passenger's seat, got out of my truck, and Peanut
walked out the front door of my trailer. He stood at the
top of the cinder block steps, spit into a paper cup, and
said, "What you know good, Mack?"

I wanted to ask him what the hell he was doing in
my house, but it surprised me it'd taken him this long to
come and see me. He stepped to the side when I came up
the steps and held the screen door open for me. He let
it slap shut behind him, and I dropped my groceries on
the kitchen table. Peanut dwarfed my small living room
but plopped all his weight down into Marshall's recliner.
The trailer shuddered under him, and he motioned at
the couch for me to sit.

I pulled one of the chairs from under the kitchen
table and took a seat in it. We sat this way until the
silence grew pregnant. It would only get interrupted by
the sound of Peanut's spit hitting the bottom of his cup.
He kept smiling at me with his best gator-toothed grin

and rocked the La-Z-Boy with the heel of his boot. He wanted me to be the first to speak and give him control, but I was willing to wait him out. I already knew he wasn't planning on killing me. He wouldn't be here if he did, and I wasn't worried about having to defend myself.

Peanut finally said, "Get anything good at the grocery store?"

"Just a few essentials."

Peanut spit. "Katie's planning on frying up a whole buncha chicken tomorrow night. She's fixing up mashed taters and collard greens to go with it. If you ain't never had her collard greens, son, you need to come over."

Peanut was right about Katie's collard greens. There was some kind of magic to them that the girl kept secret. It was something her mama taught her that would hopefully get passed on to one of her sons.

"I'd rather not impose."

"Hell, you won't be imposing," Peanut said. "Katie'd love to have you over again. She hated the circumstances that brought you over last week. It would make her feel better."

I wasn't going over there for supper, and Peanut knew it. It was just a game he played with me, and I went along. "I'll think about it."

"Do that," he said. "We'd love to have you."

Peanut leaned back in the chair, and it almost scrubbed the wall behind him. He spat a brown streak into his cup. "Talk to your mama any?"

I sat up in my chair, and my body went rigid. I didn't mean for Peanut to see that he'd gotten to me, but this wasn't a game I'd play. He leaned forward too quickly, and the springs whined. "Now calm down there, Mack. I ain't trying to make some kinda threat against Rhonda.

That's a good woman, and I wouldn't harm a hair on her head. She got worried sick the other morning when she woke up, and you wasn't at the house. I let her know you had your own business to take care of and was all right. Thank God, you didn't make me into a liar."

"I talked to her yesterday," I said. "Wanted to make sure she got back home."

"Good." Peanut spit in his cup. "Buford sure does miss her. He loved mama, but he was always jealous of your deddy for landing Rhonda."

"Peanut, I ain't gone talk about my mama that way, and I'd appreciate it if you didn't either."

He nodded at that, and then his tone grew more serious. "Your brother's madder than hell at you. He's talking like he don't wanna have nothing to do with you no more. I've tried to get that outta his head, but he don't wanna hear it. He took it real personal that you went rogue like you did."

I knew Peanut wanted me to play into the drama with Marshall, but he could stay mad at me. This wasn't the first time he said he didn't want to have nothing to do with me. It might be a few months before we ever spoke again, but we'd mend this bridge.

"What've you done with my brother?"

Peanut didn't dance around the question like I thought he might. "I got him and Caudell working a job up in Memphis."

That was good. I didn't have to worry about Marshall so much if he was with Caudell. It meant Peanut was serious about him working for him, and he wasn't getting put directly in harm's way. It also meant, if either of them needed to take a fall, it would be Marshall who took it. He'd end up in a cell in Sweetwater right next to Deddy.

Peanut said, "Now that we got the pleasantries outta the way, I need to remind you of your debt. It's even larger than it was, Mack, because I had to save your ass again. You got reckless over at that church and left a damn warpath behind you. On the one hand, I appreciate it because I ain't gotta worry 'bout the preacher now, but Darryl Tracy was damn near ready to throw you under the jail. I can't have that with you already owing me like you do. Taking off on me like you did the other night doesn't help your case any and puts you even further in the red. On top of all that, I pinned that preacher's murder on two of my boys to keep Darryl Tracy off your ass. That puts you squarely in the loss column, Mack, and I own you for the foreseeable future."

"You don't own shit, Peanut."

"Now ain't the time to be mouthy. Just know that when I come calling, you drop whatever it is you're doing and do whatever I ask. I'm your top priority now, Mack. Until I say otherwise."

Peanut leaned forward and used the arms of the chair to boost himself out of it. He checked the time on his watch and said, "I gotta be going. Katie asked me to pick Ray up from baseball practice. That boy's gone be good, Mack. Gotta helluva arm on him. You oughta come see him play sometime."

Peanut smacked me on the shoulder as he made his way toward the door and then stopped. "In case you're wondering, I pinned that preacher's murder on Wiley and Tommy. Them boys was underperforming, and I was looking for a reason to get rid of 'em. At least you did me that favor." He opened the screen door, and before it smacked shut behind him, he said, "Be seeing you around, Mack."

11.

Mama stopped in to check on me late one afternoon. I sat on our trailer's redwood deck, drinking straight from a bottle of bourbon, watching the horizon change colors. Mama sat down in the rocking chair next to me and watched me drink. It wasn't until I sat the bottle off to the side that she spoke.

"You're drinking too much, Mackenzie," she said, her tone a flat rebuke of my problem.

"Don't come over to my house and start in on me like this, Mama. I ain't in the damn mood for it."

"You ain't in the damn mood for nothing no more, son."

"Mama, I'll go back in the house and lock the door."

"I'm just worried about you."

"They ain't nothing to be worried about. I can quit drinking any time I want.'"

"Now's as good a time as any."

"I wish it was."

We got quiet, and the cicadas filled our silence with their summer chorus. Albermarle Mountain's radio towers blinked on and shined the way the North Star did for the wise men who searched for Jesus. Mama watched them along with me.

"I talked to your brother yesterday," she said, looking away from the blinking lights and back at me.

"Yeah? How's Marshall doing?" The topic of my brother made me want to reach back for the bottle, but I resisted the urge.

"You'd know if you ever called him."

"He don't wanna talk to me," I said, really wanting another drink.

"How long're you gonna go without talking to him, Mack?"

"Until I'm ready."

"It's been months now."

"And it'll be a few months more."

"You two're just as damn stubborn as your Deddy," she said. "I'd choke him to death if I could get my hands on him." Mama wrung her hands together like she had Deddy's windpipe in her fists now.

Hearing Mama's idle threats finally sent me back to the bottle. I reached down, grabbed it by the neck, and took a hard pull from it. The bourbon burned going down and brought tears to my eyes. I wasn't entirely sure if they weren't just from my depression, and it was the only way they could get released. Mama did speak after I started drinking again. She sat with me until the horizon got dark and then left without saying goodbye.

If I were being honest, I saw my brother's face every time I reached the bottom of a bottle of Woodford and thought about calling him every time I took another swig of beer. More than once, I found myself standing over the house phone with the receiver in my hand. The dial tone brought me into the present each time, and the phone felt like holding a burning piece of coal. I'd slam it back onto its base and go back to drinking. I didn't even know what number I'd call. Peanut gave me no way to contact Marshall, and I was too prideful to ask Mama. There was his cell, but I deleted the number.

Nightmares kept me up all hours of the night. Andrea came to me in them, naked but covered in scales and her eyes held the same emptiness as the copperhead. Her words came out a hiss, and her tongue darted between her jagged teeth. Sometimes in the dreams, the preacher would accompany her. He'd be in his Sunday best, carrying his worn leather Bible under his arm. The hole I put in his head shined a blinding light everywhere he cast his eyes. Andy always twisted before him and became a writhing serpent. Randy Jessup took her up to dance. He'd hold her out at arm's length and twist and spin and shout praises in tongues. I'd jerk awake and reach for an unopened can of beer every time.

ACKNOWLEDGMENTS

Writing may be a solitary practice, but the publishing process is not. Readers would not be holding **A Violent Gospel** in their hands right now without me getting a whole lot of help along the way. There's a long list of folks I need to thank. I'm not going to remem-ber them all, but I'll do my damndest. If you don't see your name here, just know I couldn't have written this book or got it published without you. I'm grateful.

First, Ron Earl Phillips. Not only did you read this book and give it a home, but you designed one of the most badass covers a book has ever gotten. Thanks for taking this book out of the trailer park and putting it on shelves. None of this happens without you. Let's do it again sometime. Whaddaya say?

David Tromblay, you helped me tear apart the first draft of this book and make it into something good. I appreciate you taking me under your wing and giving me a crash course in writing. I've learned more from you than any book on the craft. I appreciate your friendship and hope there are other books we get to rip apart and book back together.

Bobby Mathews, that damn synopsis wouldn't have gotten written without you, bud-dy. I appreciate the hell outta that. I don't have a lot of good to say about Alabama fans, but you're one of the good ones. I'm drinking you under the table at our next Noir at the Bar.

Brian Panowich, not only did you say so many kind things about my book, but you went out of your way and promoted it in a way I never could have. I will be forever ap-preciative of you taking out that ad in Mystery Scene. All I asked for was a blurb, and you swung for the fences. If I haven't already bought the first round by the time you read this, I hope I get to do it one day soon.

To the other writers who blurbed my book, thank y'all so much for taking the time to read my little book. It's a damn good feeling to see something I wrote get the kinda praise it did from writers I've looked up to for so long. Hope I get to return the favor one day.

To all my family and friends who have believed in and supported this dream. There are too many of you for me to list but just know this book doesn't exist without y'all.

Finally, to Dawn, nobody has loved me, supported me, believed in me, and given me as much creative space as you have. Every single word in this book belongs to you. You read it before anyone, gave me the confidence to send it out, and made me cut that dick joke that went a little too far. It was the right call. Thank you for sacrificing all those early morning cuddles so I could get up and write. I love you more!

Mark Westmoreland is a Georgia native who lives in Oklahoma with his wife and two dogs. He's a full-time Dawgs fan with a sideline as a writer. Sippin' bourbon and watch-ing Burt Reynolds are two of his favorite pastimes. *A Violent Gospel* is his debut novella. You can find him hanging out on Twitter @ItsMarkY'all.